SAMMY
and the
EXTRA-HOT
CHILLI
POWDER

To

Hector
Best Wishes,
Charlie

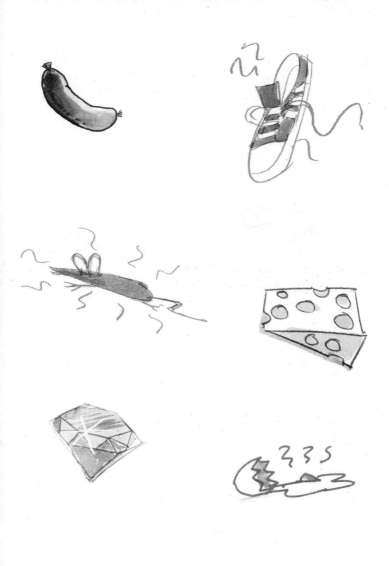

Books by Charlie P. Brooks

The Super-Secret Diary of Holly Hopkinson

THIS IS GOING TO BE A FIASCO

A LITTLE BIT OF A BIG DISASTER

JUST A TOUCH OF UTTER CHAOS

CHARLIE P. BROOKS

Illustrated by Steve May

HarperCollins *Children's Books*

First published in the United Kingdom by
HarperCollins *Children's Books* in 2024
HarperCollins *Children's Books* is a division of HarperCollins*Publishers* Ltd,
1 London Bridge Street
London SE1 9GF

www.harpercollins.co.uk

HarperCollins*Publishers*
Macken House, 39/40 Mayor Street Upper
Dublin 1, D01 C9W8, Ireland

1

ISBN 978–0–00–859748–1

Charlie Brooks and Steve May assert the moral right to be identified as the
author and illustrator of the work respectively.

A CIP catalogue record for this title is available from the British Library.

Printed and bound in the UK using 100% renewable electricity at
CPI Group (UK) Ltd

This book contains FSC™ certified paper and other controlled
sources to ensure responsible forest management.

For more information visit: www.harpercollins.co.uk/green

To Deborah – a true lover of all animals

SAMMY

HARRY

BEANIE

PROLOGUE

I'm Sammy, and I live with Beanie and Mrs Brown in a café in the Cotswolds. I have a lovely life with them here, so I am a lucky puppy. You see, there are lucky puppies and there are unlucky puppies. And I guess I definitely belong to the first category . . . but it was a very near miss.

Can I tell you how it all started? Well, Susie, Santiago and I were the products of a surprise romance between my dad and my mum. He was a rather dashing Irish setter from the wrong side of town with a smooth gallop to him and a flowing mane of red hair, and my mum was a very intelligent but rather high-maintenance poodle who didn't move anywhere in a hurry and never had one of her neat black curls out of place.

They met in the bushes of Regent's Park in London. Mum was from a well-off family who lived in an immaculate house up on Primrose Hill. It was most unlike her to get chatting to such a chancer as Dad. I just don't know what she was thinking!

Anyway, it was all a terrible shock to Mum when she discovered one morning that she was now the mother of three crossbred puppies. I think she was relieved that no more had popped out, to be honest with you. But obviously she wasn't going to keep

us – that would have been TOO embarrassing for the human family.

The first woman who came to buy us smelled shockingly awful. She must have sprayed herself with dog repellent before she left home. Disgusting wafts of lavender and roses . . . ugh. Those sorts of perfume smells DO NOT appeal to dogs. What sort of person wants to walk around making everyone sneeze?

She had a long neck, a sharp voice and a pointy nose, which was turned up as if even she didn't like the smell of herself.

This woman came from the same part of town as Mum. And all she wanted was a pampered poodle. One that would be too fancy to poo as they walked around the park on Sunday mornings. I just couldn't see this lady bending over in her Sunday best, pushing 'doings' into a black plastic poo bag.

No. She just wanted something decorative to trot haughtily beside her. And I was not that dog, OK.

So, thank goodness, she took my sister Susie – she would be just fine at that job. As long as she didn't gallop around like Dad when things got exciting.

The second visitor was a plump man with a red face who smelled jolly nice; like a mixture of rotting fish, socks, cow manure and body odour.

Yummy!

But I heard him mutter that dogs should be kept lean and mean and worked hard. So he had come to the WRONG house as far as I was concerned. It was probably the Irish setter blood that had attracted him to us.

Well, thankfully he picked my brother Santiago and NOT me. He was going to grow up to be some sort of hunting dog. Poor Santiago. Although, at least he'd get to live in a house that smelled nice.

Once Susie and Santiago had got their bums out of my face, I was the only one left when Harry came calling. Lucky Harry!

Happily, he didn't smell too bad – just a hint of old bananas – and he looked fit and strong, so probably good for taking me on nice long walks. I turned my puppy-dog eyes on and gave him a few blinks, making my eyelashes as long as possible. After all, you've got to play every card you're dealt.

For a moment, I didn't think he'd take me. But what I didn't know was that Harry was determined to have a partner who was out of the ordinary.

Harry, you see, had spent all of his life in the Army's Bomb Squad, working with labradors, and now he wanted to try something different. He was happy to take a chance with me: a weak-looking, leggy, red-coated setterpoo with big clumsy feet.

The next thing I knew, I had said goodbye to

Mum and I was sitting in Harry's lap, and we were driving off down the road away from Primrose Hill.

Halfway home, Harry said, 'You're very gentle, but I think you're quite spirited . . . so I'm going to call you Sammy, after my best friend.'

I didn't want to ask if his best friend knew about their namesake. Or if they'd mind.

But it all sounded pretty good to me. After all, people don't name their dogs after their best friend one day, and then chuck them out on to the streets the next. Do they?

CHAPTER

1

The great thing about living with Harry was that he just wanted to play hide-and-seek all day long. We spent weeks goofing about and I soon got pretty good at it. Goofing around, that is. So you could see how lucky I was without looking too hard. Not many adults are up for playing ALL DAY.

To start with, the games were really easy. Harry would let me sniff a nice smelly old shirt of his and then he'd hide it under a box on the lawn.

'Sammy . . . use your instincts, not just your sense of smell,' he'd tell me.

There were always four boxes, painted in different colours: blue, red, yellow and black. It didn't take me long to work out that blue was Harry's favourite colour.

Anyway, the shirt was deliciously, **STONKINGLY** well worn, so it was VERY obvious which box it was hidden under. I could smell the scent particles on it from my basket inside the kitchen. But I don't think Harry realised quite how easy it was for me, because every time I got it right, he gave me a sausage. And then he'd let me tear the shirt to pieces. A win-win in any puppy's book.

But after a while, I thought to myself, *Sammy, you've got to smarten up here . . . If he realises just how easy this is, he won't give you a sausage EVERY time.* So I dragged things out a bit now and again to keep him guessing.

Although Harry was super good fun and up for rough and tumble when we played games outside, when we were inside our house he was a bit . . . well, a bit tidy. And rather fussy.

I'll give you an example. He had this thing about shoes and slippers. He always liked them sitting next to each other. So whenever I took his right shoe and put it in the kitchen and then moved his left shoe into the bedroom, he'd go around collecting them up and then put them back together again. How funny is that?

I mean, what a waste of time. After all, shoes don't mind if they're not together the whole time. Even if they do miss each other's pong, I should think they're only too happy to have a bit of 'time-out' from each other.

And he was just as weird about gloves too. Did it really matter if a few fingers were missing here and there? It wasn't that cold where we lived. And while we're on that subject, his scarves worked perfectly well with a few holes in them too.

But Harry never got really angry at me for messing around with his things. He'd just say, 'Ohhh, Sammy . . . really? . . . Why that one? It's my favourite.' So I think it's fair to say that he had a **MASSIVE** obsession with tidiness.

If you want another example, take that time with the sofa. We'd been out for a long walk in the park in the rain – which included a sneaky roll around in some gorgeous fox poo that Harry didn't spot – and when we got back I hopped on to the sofa for a little rest, but Harry got

so overexcited I thought he'd put his fingers in the toaster.

'Oh no!' he shrieked. 'Not the sofa, Sammy – you're covered in mud! And . . . oh no . . . you stink. What have you rolled in?'

The bloomin' cheek of it. *Keep your pants on,* I thought. *It will brush off.*

And anyway, I had quite a lot else to put up with in our house too. Because there was always a constant stream of dreadful stinks attacking my nose.

To start with, there was the bin in the kitchen.

WHOA!

Harry disinfected the kitchen bin twice a day. As soon as it started to give off any nice aromas, BLAM – Harry was in there squirting smelly stuff all over it. It was enough to make you want to vomit.

And then there was the basket in his bedroom where he put his dirty clothes, which first he folded neatly. (Folding up dirty clothes isn't normal behaviour, is it?)

PHWOAR!

In the house on Primrose Hill where I was born, I could often sniff a few smelly socks, the odd sweaty shirt, some mouldering pants and even an occasional damp towel. But not in Harry's house. No, here we had a special odour-absorbing laundry basket that smelled of fake chemicals. I'd rather have shoved peppers up my nose than lie down next to that thing.

The worst hazard of all, though, was our bathroom. You only needed two words to describe that nose torture chamber. Soap and shampoo.

EUCH!

At night I was meant to sleep in my basket in the kitchen. But sometimes I would sneak upstairs and jump on to the bed and snuggle up next to Harry, and as he gave me a lovely stroke he would say, 'I don't think you should really be sleeping here, Sammy.' I would then pretend to be fast asleep so he couldn't make me go downstairs. And then he would say to himself, 'Oh well, I don't suppose it will do any harm.'

After a few months, our games started to get a bit more complicated. Or so Harry thought. But really I was just playing along.

One time, for instance, he got a lovely old sock and he hid it on top of a wheel on his car. But when he gave me the other sock to sniff, full of the magnificent aroma of old skin, I could also smell the car tyre scent on his hand, which gave the game away. And his eyes kept flicking towards the car anyway. He needed to start controlling them if he wanted to win any of these games.

You might think that I was cheating by watching his eyes when I was meant to be using my nose. But he had told me to use my instincts. And that included observing things and noticing what was going on.

Anyway, I made a big deal of hunting all around the garden, sniffing here and there, looking behind walls and so on. This was all just to give Harry a bit of excitement before I wandered breezily over to the car and got the sock for him in exchange for my sausage.

During the summer, we would go out to the park very early every morning before anybody else was about.

I was desperate to chase the dustbin squirrels and the doofus ducks. All that squirrels do, according to Harry, is chew the bark off trees. I actually like the squirrels because they squirt lovely-smelling stuff out of their bottoms everywhere.

We always had the place to ourselves, which was terrific. But once the winter closed in, we played most of our games in the garden. This was a real shame because the butcher's shop was on the way home from the park and it smelled of blood and guts and tripe.

LOVELY.

I think the spring crocuses and daffodils had started appearing when I really outfoxed Harry one morning in the garden. And he totally made QUITE a spectacle of himself.

What happened was that I decided we would play our games in reverse. In other words, I would do the hiding and he was to do the finding.

Obviously, I wanted him to try as hard as possible. When he wasn't looking, I chose his favourite pair of trainers and took them to the garden. Not because they smelled terrific, but because I knew Harry, in his strange way, would be desperate to reunite them.

I hid the left shoe in the garden. Well, buried it, actually, quite deep in the compost heap. And then I gave him the right shoe and barked some encouragement.

'Oh no, Sammy, not my trainers,' he said in a very agitated manner.' So I just kept barking until

he got on with the game. I started to feel terribly sorry for Harry that day. I know now that he's basically got no sense of smell AT ALL. Imagine going through your whole life and not being able to pick up the scent of a trail. How on earth does he find anything? I guess that's why Harry got so upset when he couldn't locate his missing trainer. But I thought it was good to keep encouraging him, so I left it buried in the compost heap.

It's still there. I'm sure he'll sniff it out soon.

I don't know whether it was to get back at me for burying his trainer, but Harry soon pulled a stunt on me that I was massively unhappy about.

The day started harmlessly enough. We had a nice early walk, I chased a few nerdy cats and a juicy dustbin-smelling squirrel, and then, just as we were eating our breakfast, Harry casually said, 'Right, Sammy, it's time to meet your new friends.'

New friends? I thought. *What new friends?*

I was NOT happy. We – that is, Harry and me – were getting on nicely by ourselves. Why did we need any new friends?

I didn't think Harry really liked other people that much. He certainly seemed to be very shy when people tried to talk to him in the park. He was much happier when we were at home watching TV together. So I was confused as to why he wanted to meet some 'new friends'.

Anyway, I presumed that we'd just go to the park to meet them. And that we'd go there when people who smelled interesting might be up and about.

So I knew something was wrong when he told me to get into the car. And, to make matters worse, I had grown too big to sit on his lap.

Harry was very quiet in the car. Normally I'd put my feet on the dashboard and we'd listen to the radio and have a bit of a sing-along together, but that day there was none of that. I could sense that he was uneasy. Then after half an hour we pulled up outside a building.

There was a big sign on it that said: 'Border Security Dog Unit'.

Not a bloomin' park in sight.

'Come on then,' Harry said in a false-cheerful voice I hadn't heard before. 'Let's go.'

Go where? I wondered, as we entered the building, which smelled like Harry's bathroom. Not a place to spend more time in than you had to. And I could sense that Harry was still a bit nervous.

What a ginormous, gargantuan shock I got. The room was full of cages. And some of them contained other dogs! And then Harry stuffed me into one of them.

'These kennels look nice . . . and you're going to

make some new friends,' he said. I gave him a look that said, *Well then, why don't YOU crawl into one as well?*

Really, what did he think he was up to?

Harry looked a bit flustered, gave me an apologetic pat – no eye contact, by the way – and then went to talk to a bunch of people standing in the room wearing fluorescent jackets.

CHAPTER 3

'How are you doing, Harry?' a man who turned out to be called Sergeant Sourman asked, with a smirk on his face. 'So that's Sammy, is it?'

I happen to have unusually good hearing, so I could hear every word that man in his silly Day-Glo yellow jacket was saying. And I am not a 'that'.

'Sure is,' replied Harry. 'And Sammy's good, really good.'

'Well, it's going to be interesting,' Sourman continued.

'Of course, it won't be the same as the training we've done at home,' Harry said. 'Come to think of it, I'll miss having her at home.'

Hang on, I thought. *What does he mean . . .* 'miss having me at home'? And what was this 'training' Harry was talking about? I was beginning to feel very uneasy. I was not enjoying my day out.

And then a few of the other fluorescent-jacketed people started making rude remarks about me. One of them said they didn't like my sleek long red coat; another said I looked too skinny; some idiot said I was too long; and another dumbo thought I wouldn't be able to take the work.

WORK? WHAT WORK?

Harry had never said anything about WORK.

The dog in the cage next to me had a mournful

look about him. His eyes were watery and he had folds of skin hanging down from his cheeks and a bit of slobber dripping from the corner of his chops.

'I'm Dolby,' he said in a slow drawl. 'You're an unusual-looking dog.'

'Excuse you, Dolby,' I replied. 'Have you looked in the mirror recently? You're not exactly up for winning a beauty contest yourself.'

'My family have been trackers for generations. Everyone knows that bloodhounds have the best noses. I can give someone a day's start across open country and still track them.'

'Well, bully for you,' I replied. 'I hope they keep you busy.'

'Actually, things have been a bit difficult recently. Too much perfume wafting around the airport and not enough runaway people fleeing across fields.

So, what sort of dog are you, anyway?'

AIRPORT? Did he say 'airport'? I wondered, before replying proudly, 'I'm a setterpoo, from North London.'

'A setterpoo?' barked a spaniel in the cage on the other side of me. 'More like a mongrel . . . Did you hear that, everyone? Harry's been training up a mongrel.'

'I beg your pardon,' I said defensively, 'I am not a mongrel. I'm a crossbreed, and we are VERY intelligent and level-headed, unlike you excitable spaniels.'

'Excitable . . . EXCITABLE . . . **EXCITABLE!** Did you hear that, everyone?' the spaniel barked, as he started tearing around his cage trying to catch his tail.

'I'm one of the best in the business – nothing gets past me. Don't get me started, you, coming in here and upsetting me just when I'd calmed down.

'The cheek of it, winding everyone up and calling ME excitable! You tell him, Sepp.'

'You've upset Spike now,' growled a German shepherd in the cage opposite, who was presumably Sepp. I didn't like the vibe from him one little bit. His teeth were protruding out of the side of his mouth, and there was a distinct aura of badness shimmering around his head. He was as mean a dog as I'd ever seen.

'I was just saying . . .' I began.

'Well, don't. We don't need amateur mongrels causing trouble, do we, Petunia?'

Petunia was looking at me with an aloof, disinterested expression. She was an English pointer with small eyes and a fancy, metal-studded pink collar.

'You won't be joining our gang, mongrel, or crossbreed . . . or whoever you think you are,' she said. 'So I suggest you just keep quiet. Or else.'

After the most boring wait of my life, Harry came back and let me out of my cage. And we headed for the door. *Phew*, I thought. *Fresh air.*

Crazy Spike followed us, along with another man. Doleful Dolby just gave me a bored look, and Sepp, who was clearly the kennel bully, said something rude under his breath, which I chose to ignore.

Harry stank of coffee. How dare he party while

everyone was being mean to me! I was going to hide a lot more than his favourite trainers when we got home. No sirree, I wasn't going to let Harry forget this morning for a long while.

But I had to forget the prospect of fresh air. Instead, Harry took me into a massive shed that had every smell in it I'd ever come across – and a lot more besides.

Spike was shaking with excitement. A bit like I did once when I ate a whole box of Harry's Coco Pops. *Spike needs to think carefully about his diet,* I thought, *because he must be eating way too much sugar.*

And then Sergeant Sourman said, 'Right, let's get started.'

Spike was given a cloth to smell, and then, straining on his lead, he went charging around.

From where I was sitting, I could smell the

sweetness of the scent on the cloth. And I could also tell where the same smell was located in the shed. But Spike went tearing off in the wrong direction.

I should have told you that the weird thing about this shed was that it was completely full of suitcases and packages spread around all over the place.

Very untidy.

It was definitely nothing to do with Harry. He'd have stacked everything up in neat piles.

Spike was scampering all over the suitcases with his sharp claws. Whoever the suitcases belonged to was going to be furious when they turned up to collect them.

After a few minutes, Spike finally found the sweet smell by one of the cases, came to an abrupt halt, and sat down next to it, panting heavily.

His handler was given the thumbs up by the fluorescent-jacketed Sergeant Sourman and Spike was given a biscuit. Probably with even more sugar in it.

'Good boy, Spike,' his handler said, giving him a pat.

'Excitable, am I?' Spike snorted as he went to unwind at the back of the shed. 'Excitable, indeed . . . I'll take you down any time you like,' he warned, blinking furiously.

'Come on then, Harry. Bring that mutt forward,' Sourman shouted, pointing at me.

'Mutt'? I thought to myself.

RUDE.

'Come on, Sammy: concentrate, now. Don't let me down,' Harry muttered under his breath. He got very geed up, did Harry, when it came to these games.

Then he gave me a cloth to stick my nose into. It was a different colour from the one Spike had had and it smelled DISGUSTING. I mean bitter, really bitter. A lot worse, by the way, than our disinfected kitchen bin. Much worse even than the chemical laundry basket.

Harry kept me on my lead during the game, which was a bit of a cheek. Something else we would have to discuss when we got home. But he let me choose where the scent took us. Which was not pleasant, I can tell you.

What DO people put in their suitcases? And why? The first one I had to climb over smelled like the woman who'd come to take Susie away. Maybe she and Susie would be turning up later to collect it.

The second suitcase smelled much better. It must have contained some really well-worn socks.

And I think the one after that had some animals with bad tummies in it. Very exotic indeed.

Anyway, it only took me a couple of minutes to find the horrible, bitter smell. It was over in the far corner of the shed in a black bag, ponging like anything.

'OK, that was pretty good, Harry. Maybe beginner's luck?' Sergeant Sourman suggested.

Harry seemed very pleased as we walked away. I thought we'd be heading back towards the car – except he was walking straight down the corridor, back towards the door leading to the cages.

'Hang on a minute, cowboy,' I said going into reverse. 'I don't fancy going back in there.' So I sat down and rooted my bottom to the spot.

Harry gave a jerk on my collar, which he hadn't done since I was a puppy.

I shook my head and cocked my ears, as if to say, *Hey, cut it out, Harry*. But he wasn't zoning in on me.

'Sorry, Sammy. You've got to stay here. Now, don't let me down. I'll be back tomorrow and every day after that. We're going to be a great team.'

Huh. Some team player Harry was turning out to be, dumping me in a cage with a miserable bloodhound, a scary German shepherd, a wild spaniel and an aloof English pointer for company.

CHAPTER 5

The next few weeks were just terrible. I was so, SO, SO homesick. Imagine living happily in your home and then WHAM – you're sent off to stay with strangers who are horrible to you. And picture all that going on in a shed that smells like someone's bathroom. Not nice, I can tell you.

Petunia was the meanest. Being given the cold shoulder by an English pointer, when your only friend in the world (Harry) has semi-abandoned you, is very lonely-making. And trust me: no one does cold-shouldering better than Petunia. At first, all she said every morning was, 'Oh, YOU'RE still here, are you? Well, don't think you'll ever be one of US.'

Spike was just a pain – always trying to prove that he was better at finding things than I was. Even though he wasn't. In fact, I've discovered none of them have better noses than me. And I think Sepp knew it, because he told me there would be trouble if I showed the other dogs up.

Although I was furious with Harry, I had to admit that I was pretty relieved when he arrived every morning to take me out. And with his secret sausages in his pocket too. They smelled lovely. They had cows' intestines in them and some other bits too, and they reminded me of the nice tripe smell from the butcher's shop around the corner from our home.

We didn't go for nice walks around the park any more. Oh no. Every day we just played the same 'find the cloth' game, except every day in a different place. And, worst luck, always with the other dogs.

One day we went to a factory that put yummy-smelling meat into cans that had pictures of dogs on them. Harry said the stench was 'putrid'. I have no idea what that means, but it must be similar to 'delicious' or 'heavenly' or 'scrumptious'. I'd like to go back to that factory for my summer holidays.

We had to find our 'smell of the day' cloth amongst the cans.

One of the cans didn't have a top on and Petunia scoffed the entire contents of it. She might be cold and aloof, but she was also very greedy!

Her fluorescent-jacket person was not pleased with her. I gave her a triumphant look as she was bundled back into the van.

Dolby let himself down when we went to a farm in the countryside. We were meant to be looking for that day's cloth around the farmyard, which was distracting because there was lovely muck all over the place to roll in.

We went up and down straw bales and under tractors and diggers. But Dolby picked up the scent of a roe deer who had wandered past the farmyard nibbling at young trees the night before, and off Dolby went, bow-wowing in his deep voice.

His handler took off after him, but got dragged through a hedge by Dolby, who didn't stop for TEN miles.

When Dolby was delivered back to his cage that night, he seemed rather pleased with himself.

'That was more like it,' was all he said, without any regret, and then he started snoring.

Sepp really lost his cool when we visited a primary school. The kids kept pulling our ears and stuff like that (which is fine with me – they're only children after all) but Sepp snarled and bared his scary teeth at one of them who pulled his tail.

And that was the end of Sepp's school visit. Not that any of the other dogs dared mention it afterwards. Including me. I'm a setterpoo: I'm not stupid. And I'm a Pisces – we don't like confrontation.

Then Spike had a very bad day in a building called Cindy's Perfume Factory. You have never smelled anything so bad as that place in your life. It was like breathing in a combination of candyfloss, candles that smell of candle shops, and flowery things that adults spray in bathrooms after someone has left a nice whiff hanging around.

Spike completely lost the plot. He couldn't even get close to finding our 'smell of the day' cloth. He grumbled that his nose had not been invented to breathe in a chemical factory, so he was sent back to the van looking like a loser.

Now, I don't mind blowing my own trumpet here. You see, although I found delicious stenches distracting and nasty smells nauseous, I didn't let them get in the way of finding the 'smell of the day' cloth. Because I was pretty sure that the more of these games I won, the quicker I'd get back to my home at Harry's.

Even if it was making me even more unpopular with the other dogs.

'We've got to hand it to you, Harry,' Sergeant Sourman said one morning as Harry was picking up his daily smell cloth. 'She's good. Very good. Who'd have thought it? A setterpoo, of all breeds.'

Harry seemed pleased to see me every morning and always slipped me a couple of sausages when no one was looking. But that wasn't enough to get him out of my bad books. He was going to be on the naughty step until I got back to lying in front of our cosy fire, eating one of his slippers.

So, about those smelly cloths they kept making us look for in all those strange places . . . They weren't as straightforward as Harry's niffy shirts. Oh no. We sniffed out cloths with smells from really weird stuff.

Such as:

Diamonds

These actually smell of
melted cheddar cheese. Not
mozzarella, brie, parmesan
or feta cheese – nothing
like them at all.

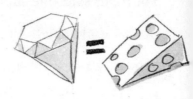

Cash

Who would have thought it,
but bundles of money smell
minty.

Explosives

Whoa! As I've already told you,
they're very bitter. You don't
want to get too many of
those particles up your snout.

Live snails

These smell very nice. A sort
of rotten adult human foot
whiff with a sweet twist.
Easy-peasy to find.

Watches

They smell like watches,
obviously, but they also give
off a very distinctive gold
aroma. I'm sure you know
that smell.

I had no idea why we spent so much time looking for these smells. I was pretty good at finding them, but it wasn't as much fun as chasing nerdy cats in the park. I was really homesick.

Harry arrived at my cage one morning looking different. As he fed me my morning treat – a couple of secret sausages, to try and get back into my good books – I looked him up and down.

He was always tidy, of course (you already know all about that), but this morning he was wearing a fancy suit and tie.

'Big day today, Sammy. This is it,' he said cheerily.

My first thought was, *Great, I'm finally going home!* And I can't say I was sorry, because I'd had enough of playing games against other dogs who wouldn't accept me into their gang.

Being excluded from a friendship group isn't nice. It's not nice even when you don't want to join them. It's just plain mean.

So there was I thinking that winning all those games had finally paid off – and I was even looking forward to digging Harry's trainer up from the compost heap as a coming-home present – when I was loaded into the back of Sergeant Sourman's van next to Spike.

What the heck? I didn't want HIM coming home to our house.

But we weren't going to our house at all. After a short drive, we arrived at Heathrow Airport, according to the massive signs on the building.

Spike knew all about this place. He told me it's where aeroplanes live. And, more importantly, it's where humans walk into them to fly off on holiday.

I was not happy. I can tell you for nothing that I did NOT want to go on holiday with Spike.

I could sense that Harry was on edge, and I soon found out why.

We WEREN'T going on holiday. We were going to play 'find the cloth' in the airport. And trust me: that's not as fun as it might sound, as I discovered over the next few weeks.

To start with, the airport smelled even worse than Cindy's Perfume Factory. It's as if hundreds of shops were having a competition to see who could make the worst smell.

There were even people going around with trolleys and spraying the sort of chemicals which Harry blasts into his kitchen bin, but spraying them

ALL OVER THE PLACE.

Then there were all the coffee shops. YUCK. What a horrible smell they made, wafting out their fumes to get everyone to buy more cups of the wretched stuff. And that coffee smell was getting all over the adults, as well as on the floor when someone spilled their drink, and all over the furniture too. It was just disgusting. Why is coffee even allowed?

Even worse, there were people going up to strangers saying, 'Would you like a free sample?' and then zapping them with a toxic liquid from a bottle.

Maybe I wasn't a lucky puppy after all. I

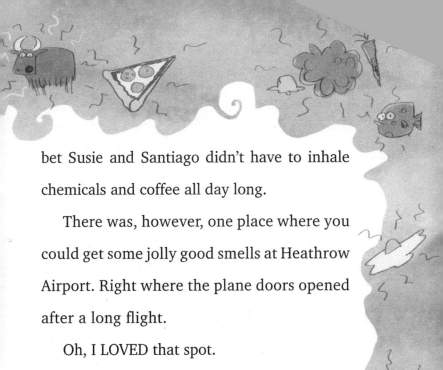

bet Susie and Santiago didn't have to inhale chemicals and coffee all day long.

There was, however, one place where you could get some jolly good smells at Heathrow Airport. Right where the plane doors opened after a long flight.

Oh, I LOVED that spot.

If you stood nice and close when the plane doors opened, you'd get a blast of warm air full of the most delightful smells.

NICE.

Harry always pulled a face and muttered, 'Phwooaarrrr!' as the aroma hit us.

It was a lovely combination of smells.

The result of hundreds of people secretly trumping out of their bottoms for eight or so hours AND not washing much during the flight. It was like a gourmet tasting menu for appreciative dog noses.

Anyway, if you put that lot together, you can see why all of the people walking around the airport ponged like anything. But that didn't make winning our daily 'find the smelly cloth' games any easier to win.

CHAPTER

7

Now we were based in the airport, our games got a bit more complicated. And it was always me against one of the other dogs from the gang.

Every morning, after Harry had given me my sneaky sausages, he said, 'Come on, Sammy, let's show the others up.'

So really it was Harry they should have been mean to, not me. I was just doing what he wanted me to do so I could get back home. I WAS NOT trying to show off or anything.

To start with, all we did was wander about to see if we could find any of the smelly cloth smells that we'd been playing with.

One day, Sepp and I were having a gentle stroll through the airport when we were taken down to the luggage hall.

The passengers off a flight from Switzerland were hanging about waiting for their bags as Sepp and I mooched around them.

At first, nothing smelled like any of the cloths we played with, but then Sepp and I both caught a waft of something interesting from a baby's pushchair.

Well, not so much from the pushchair as the baby's nappy, which was filled with some really strong stuff. Swiss people must mix a lot of liquidised meatballs into their babies' milk.

Sepp's eyes were rolling with pleasure. 'Nice,' said Sepp. 'I could follow that pushchair all day. If only we got a few more of those to enjoy.'

And Sepp was right: it was a **DELICIOUS** start to the day. A sort of breakfast-bar treat. But then something else caught my nose's attention.

Amongst the gorgeous aromas of the dirty nappy, I scented a distinct, complex gold smell. Which was not something I was expecting from a ponging Swiss baby.

My alarm bells were ringing, so I immediately sat down next to the pushchair – just as Harry had trained me to do when we'd played games in the untidy shed.

'What are you doing?' growled Sepp. 'This isn't a smelly-cloth scent. It's just a treat.'

I ignored him and gave Harry a look.

Harry seemed a bit nervous as he approached

the couple with the baby. And I could tell he was thinking, *Sammy, are you sure about this?*

'Hello,' he said in his cheery voice. 'Just a routine check. Could we pop the baby out of its chair, please?'

The couple, who were very smartly dressed, looked terribly affronted.

'That's ridiculous. Can't you see he's having a sleep?' they objected.

'It won't take a minute,' Harry reassured them.

They looked absolutely, hog-spankingly **FURIOUS** as Harry took a close look at the pushchair. Where he found nothing.

'See,' growled Sepp. 'You've made us all look like

right idiots now. Why did they ever let you out in public? A setterpoo . . . I've never been embarrassed working with Petunia, Dolby or Spike like this.'

I ignored him some more. And then I realised that the gold smell wasn't coming from the pushchair. In spite of the nappy smells pouring from the baby's nappy, I could still make out the gold scent coming from the baby himself. So I shuffled along the floor away from the pushchair towards the lady holding him.

'Keep that dog away from my baby,' the lady commanded Harry. This was a mistake that Harry immediately picked up on.

And get this. When Harry finally got them all into the search room, he found twenty expensive Rolex watches strapped to the baby's arms and legs.

Sepp was furious.

CHAPTER

8

Sepp was pretty unpleasant to work with in the airport. But he was simple to deal with if you didn't react to his taunting.

But Petunia's silent bullying coldness was a different banana altogether. She had a permanently disdainful look on her face when she watched me doing anything. Always muttering to herself under her breath.

I really didn't know how to handle her, so I just kept quiet and focused on Harry.

But Petunia, as we know, had a naughty, greedy tummy that could distract her from time to time. And that gave me the edge over her.

Take the time we were having a sniff around the passengers getting off a flight from the Cayman Islands. They were a strange-smelling bunch. But nothing out of the ordinary, until a man walked past stinking of sausage rolls.

I was standing there, not concentrating at first, thinking the sausages in those rolls didn't smell quite as nice as the ones Harry brought me in the morning.

But from the sound of Petunia's rumbling stomach, and the way she was licking her lips, all she was thinking about was eating them.

Then two things occurred to me.

Firstly, why hadn't the man eaten them on the flight for his lunch? I would definitely have scoffed them by now.

And secondly, had I sniffed a hint of mint as the sausage-roll man walked past? I thought I had. And sausage rolls do not usually have mint in them.

ALARM BELLS.

I yanked on my lead to wake Harry up, and sat down next to the man.

'You idiot! He's only carrying sausage rolls,' sneered Petunia.

'We'll see,' I replied curtly.

'So what have we got here?' Harry asked in the search room as he unpacked the sausage rolls. The man was now ALSO smelling of panic.

'Just sausage rolls,' he said, his voice quivering slightly.

'Oh, my favourite,' said Harry. 'Mind if I have one?'

And, with that, Harry tried to break a sausage roll in half. But it wouldn't break because a big wad of £50 notes was stuck in the middle of it.

Petunia just sniffed and walked off.

Spike was exhausting to work with. Always blabbering away about himself, and he never listened to a word anyone else said. And, boy, did he think he knew best about everything.

If I told him someone smelled of pineapples, he'd tell me it was actually custard. If I heard someone whispering, 'I hope they don't look through our bags,' he would say dismissively,

'They're not worth bothering with.'

It was just me, ME, ME with Spike the whole time.

One afternoon, we were watching the passport-checking hall when a flight arrived from São Paulo.

A man who was approaching the passport check looked rather uncomfortable and was making sudden movements with both hands towards . . . his 'private areas', and his eyes were swivelling all around like Catherine wheels. Way too frantic, if you ask me.

What was wrong with just quietly sniffing someone's bottom when you met them? That is, after all, an internationally established way of politely greeting someone.

Anyway, Spike and I went to sniff him out. As we walked towards him, we started to pick up a very bitter smell, which can indicate the presence of explosives.

In other words, a BOMB.

Spike started to get very twitchy. His tail was quivering like a kite's.

Well, there was a bitter aroma, but it didn't smell quite like explosives to me. There was a fleshy element to the cocktail of particles.

'I don't think it is explosives,' I cautioned.

But Spike didn't listen, of course. And like a real panic monkey, he went into full alert mode and froze on the spot like a statue. Exactly like he'd been trained to do if he smelled explosives.

Immediately, his handler set off the alarms; the armed police arrived, there were probably helicopters circling all over the place, and everyone started screaming and shouting. And I wouldn't be surprised if someone had woken the Prime Minister up if he was having a snooze.

But guess what Harry found when they took the

man from São Paulo to the search room–

FROGS.

And they were not of the explosive type.

This guy was smuggling four bull frogs through

the airport in his pants!

Poor frogs. They must have had a terrible time. No wonder they were giving off such a strong, bitter, slightly rotting whiff.

Of course, Spike thought he was a hero, even though he had misread the smell.

Working with Dolby, on the other hand, was a bit different. I wouldn't describe him as friendly exactly, but I don't suppose he's that friendly to anyone, because he's just a bit of a grump. And I really don't think airports are his thing.

I heard his handler say as much to Harry one day.

'It's time they packed this lad off to the countryside,' she told Harry. 'He's getting a bit past it for this game.'

But there's no fool like an old fool, and Dolby liked to be the boss when we were working together.

'Just watch and listen and you might even learn something,' he told me.

Well, that didn't work out for him when a flight came in from South Africa.

'Diamonds are what you need to be on the alert for from South Africa,' he told me. 'But you have to wait until they've picked up their luggage. Last year I found ten big diamonds in someone's face cream.'

'That must have smelled interesting.'

'And I've caught people with diamonds hidden in their hair,' he continued.

Unfortunately for Dolby, he was so entranced by the smell of two French ladies with exotic, semi-pasteurised brie in their handbags, that he failed to notice the niff of diamonds.

What an idiot. Brie and diamonds don't smell anything like each other. He should have smelled both.

I picked up the waft of diamonds from an old lady walking closely behind the French ladies, and it turned out that she had sewn them into her hat. Enough of them to give me a good blast. It was as if a cheeseburger fresh off the grill was walking past. I didn't get much 'watch and listen' from Dolby after that.

After a couple of months at the airport, it became pretty clear that I obviously had the best nose of all of us.

Harry was enjoying our winning streak A LOT. The sausages kept coming and I could sense that if he'd had a tail he would have been wagging it all day.

Petunia didn't take my success well. As Queen

Bee of her little gang, she must have thought my triumphs were a threat to her being seen as the kennel leader.

I could have rubbed it in her face that she couldn't smell the difference between a sausage roll and a roll of money, but I didn't. I just smiled quietly to myself.

As for the others, Sepp had been killing me with silence ever since he'd failed to notice the scent of those twenty watches hidden amongst the baby's whiffy nappy. And since the live frogs incident, Spike had spent the whole time trying to annoy me. I knew it had been pretty embarrassing for him. He kept telling everyone that Harry had helped me, and that I was a fraud.

'You wait . . . YOU WAIT . . . **YOU WAIT,**' he kept barking. 'You'll be shown up one day. Harry can't cover for you forever.'

Dolby had his own views. 'Sammy might be a witch,' he suggested in a low, lazy drawl. 'Maybe she's using magic, and she's going to put a nasty spell on all of us.'

It was quite hard to tell whether he was being serious or poking fun at all of us. And clearly Dolby wanted to leave us all wondering. It seemed to give him more pleasure than joining in the general attack on me.

Of course, what I really wanted to do was to GET OUT of that place and back to my home with Harry. But the only way I could do that was to keep beating the other dogs.

Then one morning I heard Sergeant Sourman say to Harry, 'We've got a funny one today. They want us to find a load of exotic parrots they've heard are being smuggled in. Better give the dogs a smell of this – some parrot droppings from London Zoo.'

For the record, I don't like being referred to as one of 'the dogs'. I don't go around referring to people as 'humans'.

DISRESPECTFUL.

Anyway, Harry brought the cloth from London Zoo over to my kennel. 'Here you go, Sammy. Have a good smell of this.'

I gave him a look. He was forgetting his manners. No self-respecting setterpoo goes around sniffing exotic parrot poo before eating their favourite morning sausage snack.

Harry soon got the message.

'Oh, sorry! I was in a bit of a hurry this morning and had to get them from the organic farm shop. Not your usual supermarket ones, I'm afraid,' he said apologetically.

And I could definitely tell the difference. Oooof! The organic ones were full of herbs. They didn't smell right at all.

The cloth, however, from London Zoo did smell very exotic indeed. Quite delicious, actually. I was getting whiffs of  digested rotten fruit, chewed nuts and cat widdle.

'I'll take the first flight,' Harry told Sergeant Sourman when we got to the airport. *Bit cheeky*, I thought. When Harry and I finally get back home, there'll be less of the 'I' and more of the 'we'. But it wasn't the moment to let him know that.

Petunia, worst luck, was sent along with us.

I was keen to get going and find some exotic parrots. If they smelled half as good as the cloth from London Zoo, the day would be a welcome break from the coffee and hay-fever-making smells.

The first suitcases were travelling around the

luggage carousel long before the passengers made it through passport control. Petunia and I were able to sniff the bags as they passed us.

At least, we were until Petunia got bored and said she wanted to go and check out the new range of collars in the Louis Vuitton shop. (Petunia has her handler wrapped round her little paw.) So I was left to it by myself.

None of the cases smelled unusual at first – just the normal smelly socks and underpants in need of a washing machine. But then I got a whiff of something really strong. And instead of backing away from the suitcase, like an idiot I took a massive greedy sniff, thinking the lovely aroma of rotten fruit, chewed nuts and cat widdle would come next.

Whatever I was sniffing went up my nose like a

84

swarm of bees. If I could have barked, which I'm not supposed to do, I would have done so very loudly.

OUCH.

As I shook my head, sneezing, Harry looked a bit alarmed and crouched down to take a closer look at me.

'You OK, Sammy?' he asked. But all I could do was sneeze. Harry called the customs officers over and we took the suitcase into the search room. It was FULL of extra-hot chilli powder!

Who would want to cart that around in their suitcase? Why wouldn't they just wait to buy it in their local shop like everyone else?

My eyes were streaming like a pug in a wind tunnel and so Harry took me back early to the kennels so I could sleep it off.

My head felt like it was being roasted in an oven. A scorching, fiery, red-hot oven! What was I going to do?

The next morning I woke up feeling pretty rough. The extra-hot chilli powder had gone down into my lungs and up into my head. And to a few other places I won't mention . . . And it stayed there.

The other thing I had in my head – well, in my ears to be exact – was Spike.

'So, Setterpoo, you couldn't find the exotic parrots then? Well, I did. I did, I did! Ten of them, and boy they smelled good. But I guess Harry forgot to point you in the right direction this time, huh?'

I didn't bother to answer Spike. I felt too done in. And my nose felt like it had slept in an oven.

When Harry arrived, he was his normal breezy self and he slipped me my sausages.

'Your favourite supermarket ones,' he said, giving me a pat. But something was very odd. I couldn't smell the sausages AT ALL. There was no whiff of blood. Or guts. Or tripe. Just nothing.

I suppose I should have indicated then to Harry that all was not well, but that would have meant being left in the kennels with the gang. And they were not going to give it a rest. So I decided to keep the scary situation to myself and wait and see what happened.

After all, smell wasn't everything. I still had my instincts. Harry was always telling me to use them.

Luckily, nothing out of the ordinary was planned for that morning. There were no cloths arriving from London Zoo stinking of parrots or turtles or even giraffes. You'd be surprised what people try and smuggle through airports.

Harry and I wandered around the airport keeping a watchful eye on things and then, unfortunately, we took a little trip over to the VIP (Vanilla Ice Party) suite.

A rather excitable person at the reception desk said to Harry, 'You're just in time! Guess who's over there . . . Nastasia Raven!'

Harry's a bit dopey when it comes to actors and actresses, but even he'd heard of Nastasia Raven.

'She hasn't been in any decent films for years,' Harry said dismissively.

'She and four other actresses flew in from Paris on a private plane. They were at the diamond exhibition last night – you know, the one that got robbed? You must have read about it this morning. Millions of pounds' worth of diamonds have gone missing.'

Harry just grunted. 'Don't suppose it was her private plane. I think she just played a werewolf in the last film I saw her in,' he said. He seemed much more interested in the cakes on display by the coffee machine.

'Those cakes look good, though,' he said, putting on his nicest smile for the receptionist. 'I don't suppose they've got any spare, have they? I was in a bit of a hurry this morning . . .'

So when Nastasia Raven and her four friends walked over to collect their bags, Harry was not concentrating. I could see his beady eyes were focused on a particularly yummy-looking fudge cake and a mini Black Forest gateau that were being loaded on to a plate for him.

But I was concentrating. I might not have been able to smell at that moment, but my instincts were on fire. Blazing away. And my alarm bells were ringing.

I was not getting nice vibes from these actresses.

Then I heard Nastasia sneer something very rude about sniffer dogs as she looked across the VIP suite at me. Why did she dislike dogs SO much?

Her friends seemed VERY UNRELAXED.

Then it struck me. If Nastasia Raven and her friends were smuggling something in their bags – perhaps the diamonds stolen from the exhibition they had been at the night before – then THIS was the moment when I could make setterpoos the most celebrated sniffer dogs in the world.

So I made an instinctive decision, just like Harry

had taught me to do in the garden back home. I tugged my lead out of Harry's hand and galloped across the VIP suite towards them.

CRASH.

If you have read about what happened next in the newspaper reports, I would like to point out that they got it all wrong. They covered her side of the story. No one even asked me for mine.

SCANDALOUS.

Daily Blah

EXCLUSIVE!

AWARDS DOG-PILE!

To set the record straight, I would like to point out the following:

1. I did NOT knock Nastasia to the ground. She started screaming when she saw me coming and fell over backwards in her ridiculously long, pointy stiletto boots.

2. I did NOT attack her. I just sat next to her, as I've been trained to do. And then she attacked me.

3. The blood was mine, NOT hers.

Unfortunately, when we searched their bags, which Harry insisted on doing, all we found were a load of wigs, a lot of make-up and some very elaborate FAKE jewellery.

'I'm an ACTRESS,' Nastasia Raven shouted VERY loudly. 'Why wouldn't I have wigs and make-up in my suitcase? And fake jewellery! You don't think we wear the real thing, do you?'

It wasn't hard to see how she had landed the part of the werewolf in her last film.

Harry tried to calm everything down. He explained about my incident with the extra-hot chilli powder the day before, but Nastasia would not be calmed. She was after me now. She said she was going to get me sent to a meat factory.

YIKES!

Harry had a grim look on his face the next morning when he brought me my sausages. All the spring, bounce and swagger had gone from his walk.

'It was my fault,' he was muttering to himself. 'I should have known not to take you out. I should have realised you were poorly. Look, you can't even smell the sausages. And they're your favourites too.'

'Harry, a word, please,' Sergeant Sourman said

as he walked up to my cage. 'She's got to go.'

'But she's only made ONE mistake,' Harry pleaded. 'They all make mistakes – they're not machines.'

'I know, mate,' Sourman replied, not sounding in the slightest bit matey. 'But this Nastasia Raven, well, she clearly has friends in high places and she's been making a lot of noise.'

'She can make a noise all right – I heard it. But can't someone just remind her that Sammy had a bad experience yesterday because of the extra-hot chilli powder? It wasn't her fault.'

'Oh, we've tried that. We've told her all about it. She isn't interested.'

'But Sammy has good instincts. We may not have caught her, but . . .' Harry continued in vain.

'You didn't catch her, Harry, so she isn't guilty of anything,' Sourman reminded him.

'But Sammy just made a mistake,' Harry pleaded. 'And anyway, Sammy knows when someone's up to no good.'

'Well, I'm sorry, but she's got to go straight away because I'm getting it in the neck from the top. Even the flipping Prime Minister wants to know what went wrong, for goodness' sake. I'm ringing the retirement programme right now. They might be able to find her a home.'

'A retirement home? But she's young, she might recover . . . We've invested a fortune training her, Sarge,' Harry pointed out, his voice beginning to crack.

'If she recovers, I'm sure they'll send her back,' Sourman said, and that was that.

'Well, I'll have her then,' Harry said defiantly. 'Sammy can come and live with me. And if she recovers, she can come back.'

YAY. At last! I thought. I was finally going home to live with Harry! Thank goodness for suitcases full of extra-hot chilli powder. And I would NOT be planning on making a recovery!

But Sourman was having none of it.

'Harry, this isn't a holiday. I have been given orders to retire this dog from the service, OK? You know there are strict rules on who can adopt a sniffer dog, and unless you're thinking of giving up work, you just wouldn't be at home enough to look after her properly. You know that, Harry – it wouldn't be fair on her.'

What made him think I NEEDED looking after? **IDIOT.**

I was quite capable of looking after myself. In fact, I would probably have been the one doing the looking after, and looking after Harry.

'Come on, Sarge. I can look after Sammy just

fine. My neighbours are great with dogs.'

Now Harry was really losing the plot. We didn't even speak to the neighbours.

'Rules are rules, Harry.'

'OK, OK. Give me twenty-four hours to find someone. You can't just send Sammy anywhere,' Harry pleaded.

I did NOT like the sound of this. What was going on? I was beginning to think I was the parcel in a game of pass the parcel. Maybe I was the unlucky puppy, after all . . .

Spike, meanwhile, was having the best day of his life taunting me.

'You see, YOU SEE, YOU SEE,' he shouted. 'I knew you were a fraud.'

Rather unexpectedly, Dolby growled, 'Oh, give it a rest, Spike.'

And then Petunia barked, 'Yes, shut up, Spike. If

it wasn't for Sammy, I'd be the one with my lungs full of chilli powder.'

This was not a good situation. But some moral support from Dolby and Petunia made me feel unexpectedly happy for a short while.

Oh boy, was I pleased to leave the Border Security Dog Unit the next morning. And I really didn't care where I was or wasn't going. As long as it wasn't to a meat factory!

The gang had backed off a bit yesterday and left me alone. Spike had toned down his celebrations, Sepp's simmering satisfaction had subsided, Petunia had turned off her aloof superiority, and most of the time Dolby hadn't seemed interested in anything other than the thought of deer running across a field.

I hadn't the foggiest idea where Harry was taking me now, but I was crossing my paws that it wasn't back to Primrose Hill.

Harry let me sit on the front seat of the car. And he turned the radio on and played some cheerful music. But I didn't feel like singing along, so after a few songs he turned it off.

'Sammy, you are one lucky mutt,' he said, turning to look at me. I think 'mutt' is an affectionate expression.

I gave Harry a look and tilted my head as if to say, *Really? Well, how do you figure that out? I've got half a small MOUNTAIN of extra-hot chilli powder up my nose, and you're not even taking me home with you.*

Harry drove on for a while before he spoke again.

'So, let me tell you about Mrs Brown and her lovely little daughter, Beanie,' he said, keeping his eyes fixed on the road.

I didn't much like the sound of that. Everyone knows that lovely little girls are anything but! Tiny fiends who pull the wings off ladybirds was probably more like it.

I cocked my head to the side. Harry could tell I wasn't buying it.

'Give me a chance,' he said. 'In fact, first let me tell you about Sammy Brown. I named you after him. He was in the Bomb Squad with me and he was so good at finding bombs that we said he could sniff them out. But we were clearing a minefield one day and unfortunately one of the mines got him.'

Harry looked very sad when he told me that, so I lowered my nose and looked sad too.

'Well, he was married to Mrs Brown and she is a LOVELY woman. She's said she would love to have you to stay, just until I can work out how I can have you at home. It won't be for long, I promise. She lives in a LOVELY Cotswolds village called Bloomington. You'll just love it there.'

Before I could indicate to Harry what I thought about living with a lovely woman in a lovely village in the middle of nowhere, his phone rang. It was clearly Mrs Brown.

'Harry, I can't believe you're doing this to me,' my super-sensory hearing could pick up. 'Honestly, I've got so much on! I'm just not sure I'll be able to cope.'

'It won't be for long,' Harry said, shifting uneasily in his seat. 'And think how much fun Beanie will have with her. They'll be able to go for walks together along the riverbank and be great mates.'

'Tell me about it! Beanie is half animal already.

She sure takes after her dad, and she does NOT need any encouragement. They'd probably go off exploring every day.'

'Yes, I'm sure they'll get along like a house on fire,' Harry said, pretending that he hadn't quite heard Mrs Brown's protests.

Beanie must really be one wild girl if she goes round setting people's houses on fire, I thought.

When we arrived, Mrs Brown and Beanie were waiting for us in the doorway of a café with Mrs Brown's name above the door. Harry hadn't said anything about them owning a café. That should be good for a few treats. They might even sell tripe!

'Hello, Harry. Hello, Sammy,' Mrs Brown said, using the same sort of voice that taxi drivers use when they're meeting passengers in airports.

'Gosh, what a lovely dog,' she continued, rubbing her hands nervously together. 'And quite big too.'

Normally I would have taken exception to being described as a dog, but she was obviously nervous. If she hadn't been standing in her own doorway, I might have thought she was smuggling something, so I didn't take offence.

'Oh, she's scrumptious! Look at her gorgeous

coat and her beautiful head,' said the little girl.

OK, I might have got Beanie wrong. She obviously has exquisite taste.

'So, how are you?' asked Harry, sounding a bit funny. I wouldn't have said he was worried, but he wasn't relaxed either.

'Why don't you show Sammy round the village green?' Mrs Brown said to Beanie. 'I'm sure she'd like to stretch her legs.'

Stretching my stomach with some tripe would have been a better idea, but off Beanie and I went for a walk. And I found myself wondering what it was that Mrs Brown didn't want us to hear . . .

CHAPTER
14

There was something strange about being on a lovely village green and not being able to smell it. It was much smaller than the park near Harry's house and there were no dustbin squirrels to chase.

But I had a nice time with Beanie. She's a scruffy little scrap. That day she had mud plastered all over her knees, but it didn't seem to bother her. And it was a shame that I couldn't smell her, because I bet

she had a yummy
whiff around her.

We sat under a tree
and she cuddled me a
lot. I wasn't really used
to that, because although
Harry used to stroke me
when I was a puppy, he
didn't kiss me on the nose.
But I didn't mind it.

I can think of a lot worse!

And Beanie said I was going to sleep on her bed every night.

She also told me about everyone in the village. There's a retired sheepdog called Robin, who Beanie said I could make friends with. And a cat called Mogpuss, who is a stroppy teenager. But Beanie wasn't sure if I'd want to make friends with her because she is a bit SCRATCHY.

When we got back to the café, Harry said he had to get going, but before he left he needed Mrs Brown to sign some papers.

'But I thought you were going to be her official owner,' Mrs Brown said.

I cocked my head to one side and looked at Harry. Was she referring to me?

'Yes, yes, of course. It's just for the office,' he told Mrs Brown. 'Look, it's only for a few weeks.

Just till I get all sorted out.'

Harry seemed a bit shaky when he said goodbye to me. Considering he looks like a big, tough guy, he really is a bit of a softy underneath.

'I'll see you very soon,' Harry said, giving me a long stroke. 'Be a good girl, and look after Mrs Brown and Beanie.'

What sort of setterpoo did he think I was? A guard setterpoo? Who's ever heard of one of those?

I was humongously sad to see Harry go, and I wondered if he'd ever come back. Would we ever get to live in our house together again? Or chase those dustbin squirrels? And nerdy cats?

My life was like half a bowl of tripe. But was it half empty or half full? I wasn't sure.

Mrs Brown went back to baking Cornish pasties after Harry left. I couldn't help but notice from my new basket that although she looked like she might smell rather yuckily clean, she was very pretty.

I had a very comfortable night on Beanie's bed. Although I did feel rather sorry for Beanie, because Mrs Brown had given her a horribly thorough scrub before she was allowed into it.

It was like sleeping with a saxophone, the way she trumped all night. But before we went to sleep Beanie read me the official report on my removal from Heathrow Airport, which she'd snatched when her mum wasn't looking. It didn't read well. Nastasia Raven had really turned it on when the investigators interviewed her.

'You wait and see what happens if I ever get my hands on that dreadful actress,' Beanie vowed.

Mrs Brown got up very early in the morning to bake bread and other stuff, and Beanie crawled out of bed to help her.

It was the only time of day that Beanie was allowed to knead the dough for the bread and stir the Jammy-Dodger mix: because her hands were still nice and clean after her bedtime scrub.

I noticed that she did, however, scratch her ears and pick her nose quite a lot, so I suppose some of that debris found its way into the mixing bowl. Perhaps that's what makes Mrs Brown's Jammy Dodgers so delicious?

Mrs Brown has a rather terrific organic café. It

sells all sorts of things, like bacteria and fungus, so it's chemical free. I just wished that I could smell everything.

Mrs Brown put a bed for me by the café door. She told Beanie that it was so that everyone could say hello to me. But I suspect that it was really because Harry told her I'm a guard setterpoo and can act tough if anyone is rude to her.

After breakfast Beanie and I took a wander around the village. Although 'wander' is probably the wrong word, because any trip with Beanie, however short, seems to turn into an assault course.

This is why she is partially covered in bruises and mud at all times. Between the puddles and the hedgerows, she introduced me to a few of the locals. And, boy, what a success our first introduction was – Mr Cutts the butcher at Bloomington Quantity Meats!

Mr Cutts is a very nice man. That day, he gave

me a few treats and then he said to Beanie, 'I expect Mrs Brown will be coming over to buy some tripe for Sammy.'

I may have got a bit overexcited at that moment. I don't normally jump up and shout my head off.

This was a very good turn of events. Of course, I was missing Harry a lot – but a constant supply of tripe would surely help me get over that.

YUMMY.

Anyway, Mr Cutts is also a very busy man and so Beanie said we had to go and meet Robin.

'Did I mention that Robin only has three legs?' Beanie asked casually as we walked along the road. 'He's a bit shy about it, especially with strangers, so probably best not to mention it.'

Poor old Robin. I wondered how he got about. Perhaps he had a wooden leg?

We met Robin up in Farmer Gerald's wildflower meadows above Bloomington. He was watching the sheep grazing in a field – even though he can't chase them or boss them about any more. And he doesn't have a wooden leg – and he isn't very old. In fact, he's a magnificent-looking athlete, even though he's missing one leg.

'Hello, Robin! This is my new best friend, Sammy. Sammy, this is Robin, Bloomington's finest retired sheepdog,' purred Beanie.

I was rather pleased with THAT introduction, bigging me up.

'Hello. Lost my leg,' Robin said, shrugging his tail. 'Which is inconvenient if you're a sheepdog.'

'Lost my sense of smell,' I replied, 'which is the end of your career if you're a sniffer dog.'

Then we both laughed.

'We're a right pair, aren't we? Perhaps you could

teach me to be a sniffer dog and I could show you how to be a sheepdog,' said Robin, wagging his tail in an embarrassed sort of way.

'I don't think I'd be very good at bossing sheep about. By the way, Robin's an unusual name for a sheepdog, isn't it?' I asked.

'It's not my real name. But Gerald has a car called a Reliant Robin, a three-wheeler, and when my leg got damaged in a wire fence and had to be amputated he nicknamed me Robin.'

RUDE.

But Robin didn't seem to mind.

The three of us had a stroll around the meadow and then Beanie looked at her watch.

'Come on,' she said. 'We've got to go and meet Mogpuss. Want to come, Robin?'

Robin pulled a face as if he was chewing a wasp.

'I think I'll pass,' Robin said to me. 'If you're lucky, she'll be stuck up a tree somewhere.'

So we left Robin in the meadow watching

the clouds floating by and set off back towards the village.

'Well, you two seemed to get on rather well,' Beanie remarked with a hint of mischief in her voice. 'No barking or raised hackles, anyway. He is rather charming, isn't he?'

Yup, he's OK, I thought. And he didn't seem to be too shy. I wagged my tail in agreement.

Beanie obviously got the drift as she giggled. 'I think he rather likes you.'

I hoped she was right. Obviously, Beanie was going to be my best friend in Bloomington, but perhaps Robin could become my best dog friend. My BDF, for short.

Come to think of it, I'd never had any dog friends before.

Beanie warned me on the way back down to the village that Mogpuss was going through 'a rather difficult teenage stage'.

We found her sitting in one of Mrs Muggins' apple trees. This wasn't totally surprising because Mogpuss lives with Mrs Muggins, but she didn't look that comfortable.

'Hello, Mogpuss! What are you doing up there?'

Beanie asked.

'Are you stuck?' I asked, trying to be friendly.

'How dare you!' replied Mogpuss. 'I am very offended by that suggestion. It's just typical of the way dogs stereotype cats. We've been labelled and harassed by you for decades, and it's an outrageous invasion of my privacy to ask me what I'm doing up here. It's my right not to tell you.'

It wasn't hard for Beanie to get Mogpuss's vibe.

'Oh, don't worry about Mogpuss,' she laughed. 'She's always a bit uptight when she's up her tree. She'll be all right when she comes down.'

'Don't patronise me. I know my rights! I can stay up here as long as I like,' Mogpuss retorted to me.

'Well, it's very nice to meet you, Mogpuss. I'll be around for a few weeks, so I'm sure I'll see you in the café sometime,' I replied.

After my experiences with the Border Security Dog Unit, I wasn't going to be bumfuzzled by a stroppy teenage cat.

At this point Mogpuss started to knock down apples at us, so we scarpered.

'Sorry about that. She's not normally that bad. Maybe she's had some poor exam results?' Beanie suggested.

Thankfully not everyone in Bloomington was so feisty. Beanie and I met Dr Parkin on our way back to the café.

'Hello, Jeanie,' he beamed. 'And who is this beauty?'

The strange thing was, Beanie didn't correct him getting her name wrong.

'This is Sammy. She's my new best friend,' Beanie just said proudly.

Dr Parkin is a sweetheart. He made such a fuss of me and was very sad to hear I'd lost my sense of smell.

'I wouldn't worry too much, though,' he said to Beanie. 'She might have just temporarily damaged a few nerve ends. In fact, her sense of smell could return any time. Yes, I had quite a few patients who experienced the same thing before I retired. You must bring Sammy to visit me once you've settled her in. It makes the nose tingle, by the way, getting one's sense of smell back.'

'My mum's got a bit of a soft spot for Dr Parkin,' Beanie told me after he'd gone. 'But he's terribly forgetful. Don't be surprised if he doesn't remember your name when you next see him . . .'

CHAPTER

17

You'll never guess who turned up at the café the next morning. I was right in the middle of my meeting and greeting customers that I do from my basket.

Robin.

To start with, I thought he was just passing by, but then he sat down on the green opposite the café and seemed to be waiting for someone.

After half an hour, my natural curiosity got the better of me, so I went over to see what he was up to.

'That's a strange place to be sitting,' I said. 'Can I interest you in anything from Mrs Brown's café?'

'Um . . . er . . . I'm waiting for someone,' he replied rather vaguely.

'Oh, well, she's up to her armpits in Jammy-Dodger mix at the moment,' I replied, having assumed, of course, that he was waiting for Beanie. 'And don't tell anyone, but she hasn't washed her hands since she mucked out the hens, so this batch should have a nice hint of chicken poo.'

'Ah . . . you see . . . I'm not waiting for Beanie . . . I'm waiting for—'

'Don't tell me you're meeting Mogpuss?'

'No! Are you mad . . .? Why would I be waiting for Mogpuss . . .? I'm waiting for—'

'Mr Cutts?' I interrupted again. 'He seems like a very good sort of friend.'

'No . . .'

'Dr Parkin? He's probably forgotten.'

'No, Sammy . . . I'm waiting for YOU!' and Robin went bright red, like his bottom had played a very loud note or two.

'What on earth are you waiting for me for? You might have been here all day . . .'

'Er, well, I was wondering if you wanted to come and herd some sheep . . .?' said Robin.

'But, I thought you'd retired? I mean, well, you know, you're a leg short for that sort of thing now.'

Luckily, Robin didn't seem to mind me pointing that out.

'Well, I thought I could teach you. You don't need any sense of smell to be a sheepdog. Maybe it could be a new career for you.'

It was a very kind offer, but I WAS NOT looking for a new career. I was just interested in going back to live with Harry, which would hopefully happen VERY soon.

CHAPTER 18

Beanie always got up before I did in the morning to help Mrs Brown, so when I woke I had a nice stretch, kicked a few of her cuddly toy rabbits on to the floor and thought about what I was going to do all day.

But that day something was different. My nose was tingling. And it wasn't a very nice sensation. And then I caught the stink of freshly baked bread that had wafted up the stairs. To start with, I didn't quite get it . . . and then it hit me—

I COULD SMELL SOMETHING!

Dr Parkin was right. My nose WAS tingling. I jumped out of bed and ran down the stairs to let Mrs Brown and Beanie know what had happened.

It took them a surprising amount of time to figure it out. But they finally got there when I started sniffing Beanie's feet.

'Let's ring Harry and tell him,' Beanie said, totally overexcited. But suddenly Mrs Brown looked rather serious, in a way that I'd never seen her look before. Because she had clearly thought this through better than Beanie had.

If Harry knew I had my sense of smell back, he might return me to the Border Security Dog Unit. And that would upset Beanie A LOT.

'No,' Mrs Brown said rather firmly. 'Let's not do that.'

Beanie looked confused. 'But he'll be so happy,' she cried.

'Yes, well, Harry's coming tomorrow to see us, so it can wait until then, don't you think? We can give him a nice surprise in person. Now, let's get those loaves out of the oven before they burn.'

It was clear that Mrs Brown did not want to discuss telling Harry about my sense of smell any further.

The café suddenly became a different place. Obviously I could smell the bread and the Jammy Dodgers and lots and lots of chocolate . . . which was all pretty gross, but luckily I could also smell some tripe up on a shelf somewhere.

Since Dr Parkin had said that I might get my sense of smell back, I'd been wondering if I'd want to return to the Border Security Dog Unit. And the answer was I DID NOT.

They didn't even like me there. I would be just fine here until Harry took me home. Unless, of course, I was forced to go back to the airport.

CHAPTER

19

Big excitement! Harry was coming to visit us by train. His car had broken down, so Beanie and I were going to meet him at Puddlebury station.

I thought Robin might like to come with us, but he said it was too far on three legs.

Mrs Brown was in a strange mood before we set off. She'd been thinking.

'Beanie, I've been thinking about telling Harry

about Sammy's sense of smell coming back, but to be honest with you, I'm not sure it's a good idea. Why don't we just keep it as our secret?'

'Don't you think we should ask Sammy, Mum?' Beanie asked.

'Yes, of course. Sorry, Sammy. You see, Harry might think you should go back to the Border Security Dog Unit.'

Well, I wasn't having that so I shook my tail disapprovingly.

'He can't do that, can he?' Beanie asked, getting agitated.

'Well, no and yes,' said her mum. 'It just might be easier if Harry doesn't know. Now, if you don't get a move on, you'll be late to meet him from the train.'

Harry was very pleased to see me when he got off the

train. And he gave me some Beanie-sized cuddles. Although he didn't kiss my nose. That would have been a bit embarrassing.

The footpath from Puddlebury to Bloomington had a lot of very interesting smells. Particularly past the lake where fishermen sat all day eating sandwiches while trying to catch carp.

But as agreed with Mrs Brown, I acted like a total doofus and pretended not to get a whiff of any of them as we walked back together.

Someone had left one of Mrs Brown's half-eaten Cornish pasties in the long grass by the path. It now had maggots creeping out of it and flies crawling around. I was very tempted to take a closer look, but stopped myself just in time.

I did give a rabbit a bit of a fright by chasing it along the path. After all, the Border Security Dog Unit hadn't employed me for my eyesight!

I chased it down on to the railway line. And then an interesting thing happened. The rails started vibrating. And Harry and Beanie started shouting wildly for me. When I was halfway up the bank, a train came belting by.

'Sammy! You mustn't run down on to the railway line,' Beanie cried when I got back to them. Harry looked really worried.

'Is she getting used to the countryside at all?' he asked.

'Oh, she's fine,' Beanie replied. Which was not enough information for Harry.

'Has Sammy made any friends?' he probed.

'Well, me, of course . . . and Robin, which is a bit unexpected because he's normally very shy.'

'Robin?'

'He's a sheepdog. Poor Robin. Everyone says he was the best sheepdog ever until he lost one of his legs, and now he's named after a car.'

Mrs Brown looked pleased and a bit twitchy to see Harry when we got back to the café. And I noticed she'd put some nicer clothes on than she normally wore. But she'd spoiled things by covering herself with hay-fever spray (which, of course, I wasn't meant to be able to smell while Harry was with us).

Harry had a whole heap of questions to ask Mrs Brown about me, so I sat outside the café front door and pretended not to listen.

'Any sign of Sammy's sense of smell coming back?' Harry asked.

Mrs Brown went bright red as she said, 'No, I don't think so . . . Er, no . . . no.'

Mrs Brown is not a good liar. And I would have been very surprised if Harry hadn't rumbled her.

After all, he spends his life spotting people who are behaving in a 'dodgy way'.

So I think Harry had figured it out before Mr Cutts arrived with a magnificently pongy bowl of tripe. And one waft of it was all it took to make me forget that I wasn't meant to have my sense of smell back.

I leaped to my feet and gave Mr Cutts a VERY BIG welcome ceremony, before I realised that I'd blown my cover.

Harry and Mrs Brown then exchanged a lot of words with each other.

'I'm sorry, but I really think that I should tell Sergeant Sourman that she's got her smell back. They invest a lot of money in these dogs,' Harry said in a resigned voice. 'It's my duty.'

I gave Harry a dirty look. Two in fact. One for calling me a dog, and the other for his attitude.

TRAITOR.

'Well, I don't care about your duty. Beanie will be devastated if you take Sammy away,' Mrs Brown said, sounding quite cross.

She may not have been that keen on the idea of having me in the first place, but she could now see that Beanie had fallen in love with me.

Then Mrs Brown wept a bit and Beanie appeared from somewhere and she started to wail her head off too, and I thought: *What about me? Don't I get a say in this?* So I started growling a bit and did Spike's tail-chasing thing.

Then a customer walked into the café while all that was going on and they ran straight back out again. But it did the trick. Harry agreed that it would be best for EVERYONE – including me – if I stayed with Beanie and Mrs Brown. Just for the time being.

Mrs Brown then gave Harry some delicious-smelling sausage rolls, which I don't think he would have got if he hadn't put his duty to one side.

Later that afternoon, I was interrupted while I was having a nice dream in my basket in the café. The dream, incidentally, was about a lorry full of tripe that crashed on the village green, spilling its contents everywhere.

Mrs Muggins flew in like a hurricane, causing a considerable hullabaloo.

'My Mogpuss,' she was howling, 'she's been

kidnapped!' Well, even when I'm in the middle of one of my tripe dreams, I'm pretty good at understanding English and so I'm sure she meant catnapped, not kidnapped. But Mrs Muggins didn't look in the mood to do vocabulary, so I kept that thought to myself.

'Are you sure?' asked Mrs Brown. 'Who on earth would want to kidnap Mogpuss?'

Mrs Muggins appeared to take great offence at such a question.

'She's won a lot of rosettes, I'll have you know,' Mrs Muggins replied, after making a noise like a whoopee cushion.

Mrs Brown had to backtrack fast.

'Yes, yes, I'm sure. But there might be another explanation. She might just be stuck up a tree somewhere, perhaps?'

'Are you implying she's too fat? My Mogpuss

never gets stuck up trees.'

Well, that was NOT strictly true.

'Good lord, no. Mogpuss is one of the most athletic cats I've ever seen,' Mrs Brown lied. 'Perhaps Beanie and Sammy can come to the rescue. Sammy is very good at finding things – world-famous, in fact! Particularly if she can follow the scent of something like Mogpuss's basket?'

'Basket? BASKET?' Mrs Muggins roared in horror. 'Mogpuss does not sleep in a basket! She sleeps on my bed.'

'Well, perhaps Sammy could sniff that then,' replied Mrs Brown, who was getting rather tired of all the commotion.

By the time Mrs Muggins, Beanie and I had walked to Mrs Muggins' cottage, the fire brigade had arrived and Fireman Fred was getting his ladders out.

'What on earth is the fire brigade doing here?' Beanie asked Mrs Muggins.

'I called them, of course,' Mrs Muggins said briskly. 'Mogpuss might be stuck up a tree.'

'But I thought you said . . .'

'Never mind what I said, child. Are you two going to hang around gawping, or are you going to find Mogpuss?' Mrs Muggins barked ungratefully.

So Beanie and I set to work. And up to Mrs Muggins' bedroom we went, so that I could catch the whiff of Mogpuss and follow her.

'Phwoar,' Beanie choked as we opened the door to the bedroom. 'Think I'd better open the window . . . even Robin could get his nose around this whiff.'

That was easy for Beanie to say. But I was the one who had to separate Mrs Muggins' whiff from Mogpuss's, and that wasn't totally straightforward,

although they were both
kind of nice.

I worked out that
Mrs Muggins' was a
combination of moths,
fungus and smelly feet.
Whereas Mogpuss had
an odour of slightly decaying mice and fish.

As soon as I sniffed around the garden, I found
a Mogpuss trail leading away from the cottage.
Beanie and I left Mrs Muggins wailing in the arms
of Fred and we set off across the village.

Bloomington is quite a long, narrow village
and Mrs Muggins lives near the top. The trail
left by Mogpuss led straight down through the
village, past the café and out on the path towards
Puddlebury.

Perhaps someone really had catnapped

Mogpuss and made their escape via a train from Puddlebury railway station? But that thought soon left me when Mogpuss's trail disappeared off the path and down towards the carp lake.

Beanie was beginning to have doubts.

'Sammy, be careful of the railway line. Are you sure about this? It doesn't seem like the sort of place a cat would be.'

But no sooner had she said that, than we heard a sharp 'MEE-OW' coming from an oak tree next to the lake.

There was Mogpuss, wedged helplessly between two branches. And below her were the remains of a couple of carp fish and a box of sandwiches.

'Are you stuck, Mogpuss?' Beanie asked.

'How dare you!' I heard Mogpuss say. 'You are invading my privacy. I have every right to be stuck . . . I mean, er, resting, up here. I am very offended by your interruption.'

'Oh, sorry about that. Mrs Muggins is very worried about you,' I replied.

'Well, that doesn't give you the right to share data you have about me and assume—'

'Yes, yes,' I snapped, cutting her off. 'Suit yourself then. Stay up there. Beanie and I have more important things to be doing.'

Beanie and I turned back towards the village.

'Hang on a minute!' Mogpuss shouted. While you're here you may be able to ease my descent from where I'm stuck . . . I mean sitting.' But she would have to wait until we'd tipped off Fred, just to maximise her affronted embarrassment.

When we got back to the village, there was a right commotion going on.

Farmer Gerald had an egg honesty box on the village green. The idea was that if you wanted some eggs, you put your money in the box and helped yourself. Not the sort of practice that would have worked in the perfume shops at Heathrow Airport.

Anyway, Gerald's feelings were running high. He

was mopping his brow and slapping his cap against his trousers as if ants were running up the inside of them.

'They're all gone,' he was hollering to Mr Cutts and Mrs Brown, who had come out to see what all the noise was about.

'Well, that's good,' Mr Cutts said rather enviously. 'Very good trade. If I'm honest, we could do with some of that at Bloomington Quantity Meats.'

'Yes, very good indeed,' agreed Mrs Brown. 'I wish all my Jammy Dodgers went every day.'

'No, it isn't good,' Gerald remonstrated. 'There's no money in the tin!'

'Ah,' said Mr Cutts, rubbing his chin.

'Oh,' muttered Mrs Brown. 'No, that's not so good.'

Gerald then said he wanted to call Fred, but Mrs Brown and Mr Cutts managed to calm him down.

Beanie and I joined the group and peered into the empty money box, that Gerald was unhappily circulating.

'An' I bet I know who the culprit is too,' he went on. 'The silly old fool – he'd forget to put his underpants on in the morning if he didn't wear them on his head as a night cap,' Gerald said accusingly, as he narrowed his eyes and cast a glance over his shoulder. As if the guilty party might be lurking behind a tree.

'He has been rather forgetful lately,' agreed Mr Cutts. 'He nearly walked out with some lamb chops the other day without paying.'

'Who could you be referring to?' Mrs Brown asked.

'Why, the old doctor, of course. Who else?' Gerald said with the satisfied flourish of an executioner's axe.

'Dr Parkin?' Mrs Brown asked, horrified. 'Surely not! He would never do—'

'There's no use denying it, Mrs Brown. He's got squirrels in his top meadow these days,' Gerald said, and Mr Cutts nodded, agreeing with this expert diagnosis.

Mrs Brown was being put firmly in her place. After all, she was a newcomer to the village, so what would she know?

'That's not true,' Beanie piped up, her hands planted on her hips and her chin sticking out a bit. 'And Sammy and I will prove it. Dr Parkin is a very wise man.'

I wagged my tail in agreement.

'Well, be my guest,' said Farmer Gerald. 'But I'm

telling you, I know where my eggs will be.'

So Beanie and I went to call on Dr Parkin.

We found him in his garden pruning his gooseberry bushes.

'Oh, hello, Jeanie,' Dr Parkin hailed, forgetting Beanie's name as usual as we walked up the garden path. 'Jolly good. I hoped you'd come by once Sammy had settled in. My word, hasn't her coat improved since she's been here? You can't beat the country air, you know.

'A friend of mine had an Irish setter. I remember he got her in 1966 on the same day that England won the World Cup Final . . . Yes, lovely dog. Loved tripe, you know. I can still picture her face when we gave her tripe.'

Beanie and I listened to him rambling on.

'Anyway, would you like to come in and have

some tea? I've no egg sandwiches, I'm afraid. Don't know what's wrong with Gerald's hens, but he didn't put any eggs out for sale today. Very disappointing. Perhaps they need some grit. Yes, laying hens must have grit to eat, but I expect you know that.'

Beanie and I gave each other a puzzled look and went inside for a cup of tea. Although actually he gave me a bowl of milk because I don't like tea much.

Now, I'm not proud of what we did next. But we were investigating an eggy mystery, so we had to roll our sleeves up and stick our noses into places that didn't belong to us. Because that is what detectives do.

While Dr Parkin was putting the kettle on and making a fuss of me, Beanie checked out the fridge and there were no eggs in there.

SUSPICIOUS.

And while Dr Parkin and Beanie were busy eating

Jammy Dodgers, I checked out the dustbin and there were no eggshells thrown away in there, either.

So it seemed that Dr Parkin had definitely NOT taken the eggs from Farmer Gerald's honesty box that morning.

Rather embarrassingly, I then got caught red-handed in the dustbin, because there was a nice whiff of something that had been hanging around in there for a while, and while I was investigating further, the lid fell on the floor and made a desperate racket.

'Sammy, you naughty dog,' Beanie shouted. I had to take one for the team and lie down as if I was in big trouble.

'Sorry, Dr Parkin. Sammy

learned some terrible habits when she worked at Heathrow Airport.'

'Yes, well, I'm sure she'll soon grow out of them now she's getting properly fed by you. If she's sniffing around dustbins, that means her sense of smell must be getting better.'

I nodded my tail.

'Well, funny you should say that, Dr Parkin,' Beanie said, relieved that we'd got away with our snooping. 'But you were absolutely right about it coming back. It has – she's back to normal.'

'That's excellent. Yes, very interesting. It's all about the damage to the nerve ends. A friend of mine wrote a fascinating paper on it once, but I won't bore you with the details . . .'

ne again soon, Jeanie,' Dr Parkin shouted as

we shut the garden gate. 'And keep Sammy out of Mr Cutts' dustbins,' he added with a chortle, as if he was telling himself a joke.

I gave Beanie a look as we walked back through the village. *Learned some* 'terrible habits' *at Heathrow Airport, did I indeed, Jeanie?*

Happily, things had calmed down on the village green when we got there. Gerald had gone to talk to his carrots or whatever it is that farmers do when they need to relax

But he'd left a lovely pong hanging in the air. It was hard to say exactly what its ingredients were, but if I'd had to guess I'd have said:

- **kippers**
- **black pudding**
- **stale eggs, and**
- **clothes that haven't been washed since last Easter.**

To be honest with you, the search for Gerald's eggs was an outdoor job over a big area. It was exactly the sort of thing that Dolby would have loved, but I'd have to make do without him. I wondered how the gang were getting on without me . . .

As Harry had always said, I'd have to use my instincts as well as my nose.

Not far from Gerald's egg honesty box there was a small clump of beech trees. And I noticed that the bark had been chewed on a lot of their branches.

Now, I might have been bred on Primrose Hill in North London, but I knew from the park that Harry and I used to play in that pesky squirrels like chewing trees and storing nuts near them for the winter, along with anything else that they can carry or roll.

I led Beanie over to the beech wood and, sure

enough, I could see a parting in the grass under the wooden post-and-rail fence round the trees. Just big enough for me to push through with a bit of effort.

Beanie was a bit too big for the gap, but that didn't stop her burrowing her way through the undergrowth.

There was quite a lot of grass growing under the trees, so I searched near the entrance of the 'secret tunnel'. Beanie scrabbled through the thicker stuff, and it wasn't long before she gave a screech.

'Found them!' she shouted excitedly.

And sure enough, hidden not very well under a tree that had been well chewed by the squirrels, was a nest of Farmer Gerard's eggs.

We had uncovered our thieves.

CHAPTER

22

Cracking two pretty big cases was putting Beanie and me on the map. It was as if we were running our own bureau of investigation and we were now the talk of Bloomington. Both Mrs Muggins and Farmer Gerald had been over the moon to have their lost Mogpuss and eggs returned to them.

But I was beginning to feel guilty. Because if it hadn't been for Harry, I would have spent my life walking glumly around Primrose Hill, pooing into a black plastic bag.

Harry had given me the chance to sniff my way out of Primrose Hill and make something of my life. But I was now shirking my duty to him, because there was nothing wrong with my nose any more.

Settling into a comfortable life in Bloomington might bring me and Beanie fame and fortune (and as much tripe as I could eat), but it was still a betrayal.

The problem was that I DID NOT want to go back to living in that shed with the other mean dogs. Just think what a hard time they would give me.

I decided to let my mind drift to tripe to get rid of the thought of Petunia sneering at me. But I couldn't do that for long, because our biggest case yet soon came crashing through the café door.

The case of Bloomington's disappearing broadband connection!

I hadn't a clue what a 'broadband connection' and 'broadband speed' and 'broadband bandwidth' were until Beanie explained that it was similar to a dog food factory production line.

It was all about the amount of time that it took tins of meat to travel down the wire that brought the internet to the village. Or something like that. And anybody who has ever settled in Bloomington will tell you that, however nice the village is to live in, it is UNBEARABLE without good broadband speed. Because when it's dark at night, there isn't much to do outside.

So it was a disaster upon disaster when half of the villagers lost their broadband service. It had just vanished! And one by one they appeared in the café to vent their fury.

First in was Gerald. He was absolutely furious and whiffing quite strongly. ''Tis a disaster,' he was wailing to Mrs Brown. 'I can't run my business if I can't fill in all my online forms. Someone must be using all the bandwidth. My connection just crashed in the middle of the night . . .'

'Funny you should say that,' said Mrs Brown. 'My broadband has been playing up this morning too. But surely you weren't filling in your forms in the middle of the night?' she asked unhelpfully.

'Ah,' said Gerald. 'You see, there's this website where you can meet people who don't live in the village, and I was in the middle of a conversation when the whole thing went dead. They just disappeared.'

Hmmm, I thought to myself in my basket. *If Gerald wants to make friends, it's probably essential that he does it via his computer. That way they wouldn't*

have to get a whiff of stuff that humans don't like.
Such as:

- **kippers**
- **black pudding**
- **stale eggs, and**
- **clothes that haven't been washed since last Easter.**

'And I reckon I know who the guilty person is,' Gerald said, narrowing his eyes and looking furtively out of the café window.

'And who might that be?' asked Mrs Brown. 'Fireman Fred?'

'No,' replied Gerald, failing to spot Mrs Brown's lack of trust in his investigational nous. 'It's Mr Cutts.'

'Why on earth would it be Mr Cutts? He doesn't sell any meat online.'

'No, he doesn't. But he watches a lot of films. Up

all night he is, downloading those films.'

'Really? Now how would you know that?'

'Well, I've seen him,' was all Gerald was prepared to say.

Mrs Brown had had enough of Gerald, so she asked him if there was anything else he needed, and then retreated to her bread ovens.

The next customer to come scuttling past my basket was Mr Cutts.

'Morning, Sammy. Morning, Mrs Brown,' Mr Cutts said, smelling his normal delicious self. 'Er, I was wondering . . . is your broadband working OK, Mrs Brown?'

'Funny you should ask that, Mr Cutts. No, it isn't, actually, which is a disaster for my online bakery orders. Any idea what the problem might be?'

'Well, someone must be hogging the broadband, and this is crashing the speed for everyone else. I have my suspicions.'

'And what might they be, Mr Cutts?'

'Well, Dr Parkin downloads a lot of medical journals, you know, and some of them are big documents. Perhaps he forgets just how big they are. So perhaps you could have a word with him?'

Well, Mrs Brown didn't have long to wait before she could have a word with Dr Parkin, who arrived shortly after to pick up a loaf of bread.

'Good morning, Dr Parkin. How are you today?' Mrs Brown asked.

'Yes, well, rather put out actually. I was halfway

through downloading a very important paper I wanted to look at and my broadband failed. Yes, very annoying. It's never happened before.'

'Oh dear. Do you think it might have overloaded the system, your download?'

'Oh no. I've downloaded much bigger medical studies than that before. But I have noticed that Mrs Muggins has been getting a lot of online deliveries in white vans recently – sometimes five a day! Apparently, her Mogpuss is very demanding. I wonder if perhaps Mrs Muggins is wearing out the internet?'

Mrs Brown rolled her eyes a bit at this latest accusation, and put Dr Parkin's loaf in a paper bag.

Half an hour later, Mrs Muggins came storming into the café like an express train smelling of foot powder.

'The absolute cheek of it!' she roared,

screeching to a halt. 'I just met Dr Parkin by the village green and he accused me of accelerating climate change. "Too many vans," he kept babbling. Of course, I wouldn't have to order so much online if you and Mr Cutts stocked what I needed. Really, it's too much.'

Beanie unfortunately picked that moment to come downstairs and tell Mrs Brown that she couldn't do her homework because the internet wasn't working.

Mrs Brown said a rude word and Mrs Muggins and Beanie looked very shocked. Of course, I'd heard words like that the whole time at Heathrow Airport, particularly when someone's luggage had been sent to Bogotá by mistake, but I had no idea that Mrs Brown knew one of them!

Thankfully, after a nice cup of tea and a Jammy Dodger Mrs Brown calmed down and explained to Beanie what the problem was. As if I didn't already know.

The bureau of investigation had a new case.

CHAPTER 23

Beanie started our investigation with another Jammy Dodger and cup of tea. She said that's how all detectives started their new cases. It was a bit early for tripe, so I had milk.

We made a 'Bad Service' map of the village and marked with an X all the places where the broadband was failing. And it was a very confusing picture.

At the top of the village, Gerald was having trouble, as were Mrs Brown and Beanie at the bottom.

But as Beanie and I went round the village, we found people who DIDN'T have a problem at all.

There were no complaints at the top of the village in what someone had called a Business Park (which, if you ask me, was more like a collection of old sheds with a few people pulling cars to pieces).

And the teacher outside the primary school, at the bottom of the village, said they'd had no problems (which was bad luck for the kids hoping to get out of lessons).

And Fireman Fred, who lived right in the middle of the village, said his broadband was faster than his fire truck on its way to rescue Mogpuss.

We decided to make another map, this one showing all the places where the broadband service was good and people WEREN'T having any problems.

It just didn't make any sense. We were still trying to figure it all out as we wandered back to the café to have our mid-morning snack.

Beanie had another Jammy Dodger and I had a mid-sized bowl of tripe. It smelled a bit stronger than usual – one of Mr Cutts' super-scrummy mixes.

And then we had the first MAJOR BREAKTHROUGH in our investigation. A white van pulled up outside the café, with 'Puddlebury-Whizz-Broadband.com' written on the side. But there wasn't much whizz about the portly man who got out of it and came into the café.

'Three Cornish pasties, please,' he said to Mrs Brown after he'd shuffled up to the counter.

'Everyone will be very pleased to see you,' Mrs Brown said as she put the pasties into a brown paper bag.

'Really?' the broadband engineer replied, looking

surprised. 'And why's that?'

'Well, we're having problems with our broadband. I rather thought that was why you're here.'

'Nope, I'm here for the pasties,' he replied. 'Nothing wrong with our broadband. Must be the other lot. They're always having trouble – didn't bury their cables deep enough, see.'

Beanie and I gave each other a confused look, and Mrs Brown looked a bit puzzled too.

The engineer was already tucking into his first pasty before he got to the café door. 'Ofher lot are workin' at fhe top of fhe village today . . . Fhat's where fhe pwoblem muss be fhis time,' he said through a mouthful of pasty.

So we legged it up to the top of the village. And sure enough, by the side of the road was another white van. This one had 'Chipping-Topley-Superfast-Broadband.com' written on the side of it, and it was much longer than the pasty muncher's vehicle.

'Having trouble with your cables?' Beanie asked the engineer, who was scratching his head next to a connection box full of fibre cables.

'Eh? No. Nothing wrong with our cables, no. They've been buried for years and never caused a problem. It's the other lot who get trouble,' he said defensively.

'So, what's the problem here, then,' Beanie asked bluntly with her hands on her hips and her chin sticking out.

'Er, I don't know. Everything seems OK, but we've had a few complaints this morning. Can't work it out just yet,' the perplexed engineer admitted.

While Beanie badgered the poor man, I had a quick look in the back of his van. There was a roll of fibre cable that looked just like the stuff in the connection box that the engineer was fiddling around in.

The cable smelled of nuts. Don't ask me why. It just did. What I didn't know was whether I'd be able to smell it buried underground. And that would probably depend on how deep the cables had been buried.

There was only one way to find out, so I started sniffing the grass verge next to the road. Sure enough, I could just about get the scent of the nutty fibre cable in the ground. I think the pasty-muncher was right: Chipping-Topley-Superfast-Broadband hadn't buried their cables very deep after all.

Beanie saw what I was up to, so she stopped bending the ear of the engineer and followed me.

Not only could I pick up the nut smell of the cable, I could also feel a vibration coming up from it. A similar vibration that the railway track gave off before the train whooshed past.

It was easy-peasy following the cable – but halfway back to the village, just by the track that led to Gerald's wood – the cable stopped vibrating. I could smell it in the ground, but there was no energy in it. It was as if it had died.

Lifeless.

Beanie seemed to be more interested in the track down to the wood, which was very muddy as quite a few vehicles had used it recently. Not that the mud put her off one bit.

'Let's try down here,' she suggested.

Seriously? It seemed to me like a pretty stupid place to investigate the village's missing broadband – the middle of the wood.

But Beanie was insistent.

'Come on, Sammy – take a sniff down there. Something must be going on.'

And, right enough, I could smell a cable in the ground going down the track to the wood – and it was alive.

Buzzing like crazy, in fact.

When we got to the edge of the wood, we could see a barn with a couple of cars parked outside. So we crept up and looked through one of the windows. Inside there were five men sitting at a long table, peering intently at computer screens.

'Let's go in and ask them what they're doing,' Beanie suggested. But my instinct, which Harry taught me to follow, told me that getting involved with these men would be a big mistake.

I just didn't like their vibe. It might have been because they were getting way too much screen time, but there was something evil about them.

So I did something I'd never done before. I

grabbed Beanie's coat in my mouth and pulled her away from the window, shaking my head from side to side as I did so.

On our way back to the café, where we were heading for some reviving Jammy Dodgers and a bowl of tripe, we bumped into Robin on the village green, so I invited him to come and share my tripe.

'That's a nice barn Gerald has down in the wood,' I said casually to Robin as he cleaned out the last of the tripe from my bowl.

'What were you doing down there?' Robin asked, surprised.

'Oh, we were just having a mooch about. Beanie was just showing me around, you know.'

'Well, I can show you anything you want,' Robin said, sounding rather offended. 'See anyone down there? A dodgy-looking bloke rented it off Gerald the other day; said he was going to store bouncy castles in there.'

'Oh no, we didn't see any bouncy castles,' I replied truthfully.

You may think that I should have told Robin what we really saw, given that we were probably already BDFs, but we detectives have to keep stuff that we're investigating under our collars. So I didn't tell him anything else.

My mission with Beanie was **TOP SECRET**.

CHAPTER

24

Mrs Brown was just loading another tray of Jammy Dodgers into the oven when the phone rang. The phone was within range of my super-sensory hearing from my basket, so I could listen in to what the person on the other end of the line was saying – even if they were calling from as far away as Chipping Topley or Puddlebury.

'Mrs Brown's Café, Bloomington,' Mrs Brown

said in a cheery voice. 'How can I help you?'

'It's me,' Harry said, and I could hear he sounded stressed, even though he was on the other end of a different telephone.

'Harry! Are you OK? What's the matter?' Mrs Brown asked.

'We're in a bit of a fix,' Harry said.

'What sort of fix?'

'Erm, well this is rather delicate and top secret, but I really need Sammy.'

I could see Mrs Brown's body stiffen under her floral dress.

'Why on earth do you need Sammy?' she asked abruptly.

'Well, you see,' Harry babbled, 'it's all very delicate and I'm not allowed to say what's going on, particularly over the telephone – you never know who might be listening—'

'Well, I'm sure you can tell me all about it when I next see you, Harry,' Mrs Brown said firmly. 'Must go . . . got some loaves of bread in the oven.'

And then she blinking well put the phone down.

I wagged my tail in appreciation. But then I felt selfish and guilty.

After all, I thought, Harry wouldn't be asking for me unless he really needed me. Maybe he wants my help . . .

CHAPTER 25

I heard it first. Robin's hearing wasn't as good as mine, so he was a bit behind me. And Beanie has typical 'people hearing', so she was WAY behind us.

The sound was coming from the Puddlebury direction. But it wasn't a train, it was a helicopter! It got louder and louder and LOUDER.

As it got closer, Mrs Brown came out of the café to see what the racket was all about.

'I don't know why they fly their helicopters so low around here,' Mrs Brown said to Beanie.

'For practice, I suppose,' Beanie replied, watching a massive helicopter approaching. It seemed to be heading straight for us.

By now, the noise was deafening, and there were leaves and lawn-mowings swirling around in the air.

'It's going to land on the village green!' Beanie shouted.

And it did. This massive green helicopter plonked itself down bang in the middle of the village green.

Mr Cutts came running from Bloomington Quantity Meats at full pelt, excitement written all over his face.

'Is it something to do with the broadband?' he yelled.

Nobody bothered to answer him.

Then Mrs Muggins arrived at what could probably be called a fast bustle, looking and still sounding like a giant whoopee cushion.

'Oh! My Mogpuss is terrified of helicopters,' she was bawling. 'Someone call Fireman Fred! What is that thing doing here?'

Of course, nobody knew until the chopper's engines shut down – and out of it stepped Harry.

Everyone gathered round him.

'Well, here I am,' Harry said to Mrs Brown, a sheepish smile on his face.

'My goodness, that was quite an entrance,' Mrs Brown said, looking only half pleased to see him. 'Car broken down again? Trains not running?'

'Sorry about that. No time to take the train! Time isn't on our side, I'm afraid.'

'Our side? Whose side is that? Yours and Sammy's?'

'Look, I had to tell Sergeant Sourman that Sammy has got her sense of smell back, but I didn't think for one minute he'd want to call her up. But we've got a tricky problem and even Sourman knows that Sammy on form is the best we have.'

'Did you really have to tell him?' asked Mrs Brown.

'I did. I know you're cross, but I did. They invest a fortune in training dogs like Sammy, so I thought it was only fair,' Harry said, looking sad.

The crowd was rapidly getting bigger.

'Can we go inside the café?' he asked Mrs Brown.

Mrs Brown led Harry, Beanie and me into the café. And Robin too, who wasn't to be excluded.

'So, WHAT is this all about, then?' Mrs Brown asked once the door was firmly shut.

Harry glanced down at a stand near the counter and picked up a glossy magazine. On the cover were lots of glamorous ladies who were smothered in jewels.

'This is what it's about,' he said, pointing at the jewels. 'But it's top secret. We have to keep it just between the five of us – you literally can't tell anyone.'

Mrs Brown was boiling.

'What are you talking about, Harry? And what has that magazine got to do with anything? Have you gone mad?'

'Read it,' said Harry, giving up on his apologetic voice and passing the magazine over. 'The biggest diamond display in the world is opening tonight in London to celebrate the Star of the Blue Moon at Pragnell's Emporium in Mayfair. Every celebrity who could get an invite will be there, including most of the kings and queens of Europe. And we've had a tip-off that there's going to be a heist.'

'A heist?'

'A robbery. We've had a tip-off from Interpol that someone is going to steal the Star of the Blue Moon diamond,' Harry replied urgently.

'Well, what's that got to do with Sammy?' Mrs Brown asked, standing in front of the café door like a large display of tinned fruit. Not something you'd want to bump into.

'I need her skills: her sense of smell and her instincts.'

'Well, she won't be much good to you if men in masks are waving machine guns around, will she?'

'No, but it might not be like that. Some robberies are very clever.'

'But it also might be EXACTLY like that,' pointed out Mrs Brown, not budging.

Harry looked desperately uncomfortable as he glanced at me. We hadn't even had a cuddle. But this conversation was getting nowhere. Mrs Brown was looking crosser and crosser. And Harry was looking more and more timid.

It was time for me to put my best paw forward (my right paw) and get this sorted out. I knew

Beanie would be upset. I knew Mrs Brown would be even crosser. And maybe my BDF Robin might even be a bit worried for me – but Harry needed me.

I gave Beanie and Mrs Brown a wag of my tail, Robin a wink and I went and sat down next to Harry.

Everyone knew what that meant.

CHAPTER

26

Have you ever been in a police helicopter? Well, don't bother. They are SO uncomfortable and VERY noisy. And no one has bothered to make headsets for dogs, which is ridiculous, because our hearing is much more sensitive than humans'.

I lay on the seat next to Harry and put my paws over my ears. He got the message and let me put my head on his lap. And then he put his hands over my paws.

The good news was that the pilot knew we were in a hurry, so he didn't hang about. We were up and away in seconds.

I could see Beanie waving to me from down on the village green. She had been very brave about my decision. And my BDF Robin had looked satisfyingly concerned. Mrs Brown had looked very worried too – and maybe she'd even been chopping some onions for her pasties, because she had some tears in her eyes.

After half an hour, we were flying over London – Harry pointed out Wembley Stadium as we flew over it – and then the helicopter dropped down into a massive park. That must have given the dustbin squirrels a fright.

Sergeant Sourman was waiting with his van right next to a large painted H on the grass. This was a nice welcome for Harry. But that was it. No bunting, no flags and no band. And no tripe for me!

Sourman didn't even give me a welcome pat. All he said was, 'I hope you're right about this, Harry.' If Sourman ever gets a new job, it won't be welcoming people to a theme park dressed as a giant mouse.

Harry gestured to me to get into the back of Sourman's van. And what a nasty surprise I got. Dolby the bloodhound was in one of the other cages.

'Oh, it's you, is it?' Dolby drawled. 'Surprised you'd want to get involved in all this chaos. Come across any nice deer lately?'

'Lots, actually,' I fibbed. 'Wall-to-wall deer in the Cotswolds, and they run for miles.'

'I must come and visit you one day. Anyway, it's good to have you back on the team,' Dolby added. And for a minute I thought I sensed a hint of friendliness. Although you never quite knew with Dolby whether he was being friendly or just peculiar.

'Any more info?' Harry asked Sourman.

'Nothing. We've checked the guest list and there's more security around this lot than the Tower of London. Why would anyone pick tonight of all nights to steal this diamond? It doesn't make sense.'

'Well, it will be busy . . . and chaotic. Maybe that's why?' Harry replied. 'What about the others – have they found anything?'

'No, but we've locked down all the drain covers and we've got police marksmen on the roof. This place is secure, I'm telling you.'

'I'm not sure about that,' replied Harry. I could tell that his brain was whirring frantically. 'What about the security guards? Have they been replaced? Most of these heists succeed with inside help.'

'They have,' Sourman replied curtly. He clearly didn't like the fact that Harry was better at this stuff than he was.

CHAPTER

27

Pragnell's Emporium in Mayfair was glistening when we arrived at dusk. The front of the building was illuminated with lights. The building sparkled like a diamond itself.

'We need to check the main room,' Harry said firmly to Sourman as soon as we got inside. 'I want Sammy to get familiar with the scents in the building, including the Star of the Blue Moon.'

As we walked up the main staircase, I was getting whiffs and niffs coming from everywhere. There were a lot of different jewels in this place. And they all smelled different.

The main room was like a palace. I hadn't seen so much marble and glass since Heathrow Airport. But it smelled a LOT better than that place.

'Sammy needs to smell the Star of the Blue Moon,' Harry insisted.

'Not happening,' said a stubborn security guard. 'No one's allowed to pick it up.'

'She has to get closer,' Harry insisted. 'She needs to properly connect with it.'

At that moment, the Emporium's owner, Chairman Pragnell arrived in the main hall. He was waving his arms about and barking instructions.

'That light . . . too bright . . . That glass . . . not clean . . . Those flowers . . . no . . . no . . . no! I said off-white, not CREAM. Quick! The guests are arriving any moment!'

But Harry wasn't timid.

'A moment of your time, please, Chairman Pragnell. My partner, Sammy, must get a proper smell of the Star of the Blue Moon. If anything should happen to it this evening, Sammy might well be able to find it.'

I liked his use of the word 'partner'.

'Anything happen?' Pragnell replied, his massive quiff of hair rising six inches. 'What could possibly happen? I have three cameras on the Star of the Blue Moon and my best man watching the cushion it rests on – he never even blinks.'

'I'm sure he doesn't,' Harry replied. 'But don't you think the diamond would be safer behind some bars or in a glass security cabinet?'

At this, Pragnell's nose looked like it had been

dipped in extra-hot chilli powder. His eyes spun around like underpants in a tumble drier, his ears tried to take off, and then he let out a stream of very loud noises, some of which were words and some that weren't.

'**WHOOGHHOOOOO*&£@)!±=!**' he

screamed. Or something like that. Followed by

'WHAAAAAT? Put the Star of the Blue Moon in

a cage in my Emporium? NEVER! This isn't a

prison, this is the Pragnell Emporium! We DO

NOT treat our gems like CONVICTS!'

'No, of course not. Just a thought,' Harry blabbered as the wrath of Pragnell buffeted him like a landing helicopter. 'Well, in that case it really would be wise to familiarise Sammy with the Star of the Blue Moon.'

Pragnell suddenly calmed down and reduced his voice almost to a whisper as he looked down at me.

'Oh, a setterpoo – such regal dogs. I trust them, and what a beauty she is! You're right. Guards, make way for . . .'

'Sammy,' Harry informed him.

'Sammy. What a splendid name. Would she like a snack to keep her going? Some biscuits?'

A swift bowl of tripe would have been more like it, but Pragnell didn't look as if he had one of those to hand.

Tripe or no tripe, oh boy – what an interesting

whiff the Star of the Blue Moon gave off when I got up close and gave it a good sniff. It smelled like melted cheddar cheese – a really strong one, probably Scottish, so smoky and tangy. But then there was a distinct aroma of truffle in there too – all musty and earthy. I'd never smelled anything quite like it in all my life.

'Got it?' Harry asked after a minute.

I gave him a nod. I'd know that smell anywhere if I came across it again.

Harry and I then went for a wander around the Emporium. And I got another nasty surprise. There was Sepp, making himself busy in a room full of shining red rubies, which, by the way, smell of popcorn.

I was expecting a mean snarl from the German shepherd, but I got a bit of a shock.

'How you doing, Sammy?' he asked. 'Good to see you again. Good to have you back on the team.'

I was so taken aback by his warmth that I was lost for words for a moment.

'Much better, thanks,' I eventually spluttered.

I gave Harry a confused look. But he was too stressed to notice that Sepp had been nice.

Harry and I went down the grand staircase and into the basement, where the Emporium's armoured security vaults were. And who should be there but another of my old colleagues, scratching and sniffing himself all over as if he had fleas: Spike the spaniel.

But Spike's tail wagged as if he was pleased to see me too!

'This is a nightmare, an ABSOLUTE nightmare. We need all the help we can get. And I meant to say:

thanks. You took the bullet for Petunia there, pal, when she should have been looking for the exotic parrots. It could have been her that got the extra-hot chilli powder up her nose. All good now?'

Again I was nearly speechless.

'Much better, thanks, Spike. Much better,' I babbled.

Our next stop was the staff kitchen, where Harry had a (disgusting) cup of coffee and a sausage roll. Obviously, I had a couple of sausage rolls too, but they were typical London sausage rolls – no gristly bits in them whatsoever.

And then another old acquaintance put in an appearance, still looking as if she had a bar of soap under her nose: Lady Petunia the pointer.

Initially, she looked as cold as ever, but when she saw me and started to speak, her expression softened and she said, 'Sammy, it's so, SO good to see you! You must have had such a terrible time.'

My tail nodded a bit. And then I plucked up the courage to ask what was on my mind.

'Why is everyone being nice to me, Petunia?'

'You're part of the team now, Sammy. You've earned your stripes.'

'But no one used to talk to me,' I reminded her.

'Of course not! You were a newbie back then. But you're not any more. You're one of us now,' Petunia said, giving me a flick with her tail.

Before the guests arrived, Harry, Sergeant Sourman and I went to Chairman Pragnell's office. And what an office it was! A huge chandelier hung from the ceiling, and decorative wood panelling covered the walls. And there were lots of paintings of past chairmen Pragnells in gold frames.

'We thought we should look through the guest list, just to see if there was anyone on it who might cause alarm,' Sourman said, although that had been Harry's idea.

'Alarm?' Pragnell repeated, his eyebrows doing handstands. 'ALARM?'

'Well, somebody might stand out,' Harry suggested.

There were princes and counts and earls and lords on the guest list and lots of famous film stars. And David Beckham, of course.

'Crown Prince Hans of Estonia,' Harry said running his finger down the list. 'Is he a real crown prince?'

Pragnell waved his arms around and ran his fingers through his hair, rather spoiling the work that had been done on it by the hairdresser.

'A REAL crown prince? He's not even a real Hans. But what do I care? If he buys enough jewellery from me, I'll call him a king,' the chairman barked excitedly.

'Is this the full list?' Harry asked, but Pragnell's patience had been stretched too far.

'Enough! I need to carry out my last inspection. Let the show begin! Get to your stations!' he barked as he swirled out of his office.

'That went well,' Sourman said out of the corner of his mouth to Harry.

Harry and I had been told to stand in the corner of the main room that had the Star of the Blue Moon in it. Pragnell had said that I would look suitably refined, as long as I didn't move around or sniff anyone's bottom.

The rest of the team were stationed near the front door – out of sight.

When the doors opened and the guests flooded in, they all floated in their ballgowns and tuxedos up the grand staircase to the main room, where Harry and I were pretending to be 'part of the furniture'.

Boy oh boy, were there some aromas sloshing about! Lots of different types of cheese-whiffing diamonds hanging round their wrists, popcorn-niffing rubies round their necks, and every type of hay-fever spray that you could imagine. And considering how grand and glamorous all of the guests were, quite a few of them were secretly trumping out of their bottoms as they walked around scoffing the free food and drink being served on enormous silver trays.

What was strange was that all of the decorated guests seemed so interested in talking to each other that they didn't appear to be taking any notice of the Star of the Blue Moon.

Well, I say all of the guests, but that wasn't quite true. There were three women – standing apart from the rest of the group – who WERE looking covertly at the large diamond. And I could sense some tension radiating off them. They certainly weren't joining in with the rest of the guests and eating and having fun.

I did not like their vibe.

One of those women, with bright blonde hair, was wearing a spectacular long dress covered in large blue, red and green crystals. Something bothered me about her hair, but I couldn't think what it was.

AND THEN THERE WAS AN ALMIGHTY CRASH.

The sound of smashing glass exploded around the room. Everyone turned round to see that one of the huge silver trays had been dropped on to the floor, and broken glass and spilled drinks had been scattered everywhere.

The waiter must have bumped into a guest, who was now making a terrible commotion about having drinks spilled all over her.

Harry and I looked over towards the Star of the Blue Moon – but we couldn't actually see it because the tense ladies who hadn't been enjoying themselves much were blocking our view.

Harry looked at Pragnell's security guard, the one who 'never blinked'. Like everyone else, he was looking away from the diamond, trying to see what the commotion was all about.

THEN THE FIRE ALARM WENT OFF.

I could sense Harry was worried. He whispered, 'Sammy, something's going on here.'

I felt like saying, *No kidding!* I might have been retired early, but even I could tell that something was up.

Harry and I could now see the Star of the Blue Moon again, sitting on its lovely cushion.

BUT THEN THERE WAS ANOTHER COMMOTION.

'Fire! Fire! There's a fire in the ladies' loos!'

someone was shouting. And, sure enough, smoke was pouring out from under the door.

'Come on, Sammy. Let's move!' Harry barked at me. 'We've GOT to get to the front door!'

'Nothing to worry about,' Pragnell told Harry as we passed him on the grand staircase. 'The Star of the Blue Moon is safely on its cushion.'

'Yes, but is it?' said Harry. 'I wouldn't be so sure about that.'

Then Sergeant Sourman came running up in a right panic.

'We've got to evacuate the building,' he squawked.

Harry and I didn't stop. We just legged it down the staircase as fast as our legs would carry us.

'Has anyone left the building yet?' Harry asked Dolby, Sepp, Petunia and Spike's handlers, who were all crowded around the front door.

'No one yet, but we've got to clear everyone out,' one of them replied.

Harry bent down and stroked my head.

'You ready, Sammy?' he asked. 'If my suspicions are correct, the Star of the Blue Moon is about to come walking straight past us.'

Seconds later the guests came tearing down the grand staircase, past Harry and me like a mischief of rats fleeing the fire of London. They were really trumping now, and I could also smell panic amongst all the hay-fever sprays and varieties of cheeses and popcorn.

And then I smelled something REALLY strong that started to go up my nose like a swarm of bees. But thankfully my alarm bells went off, and instead of taking another big sniff, I held my breath and didn't breathe in.

I instinctively knew it was extra-hot chilli powder.

But what was it doing in Pragnell's Emporium?

I glanced up the staircase, taking in everyone rushing towards me. And there she was, coming at me fast. The lady in the long dress covered in large crystals.

That was the moment when I remembered where I'd seen her blonde hair before. But of course, it wasn't real hair . . . it was a wig.

I stepped forward, jerking on my lead. But Harry hesitated behind me.

'Get that dog away from me!' the woman shouted in a familiar voice.

Nearly hidden by her dress, her hand was holding a small perfume bottle low to the floor. But she wasn't spraying perfume. It was extra-hot chilli powder! And then I felt a sharp pain in my shoulder as she drove her stiletto shoe into me, knocking me back.

'Control that dog, Harry,' Sourman shouted over.

'She's getting in the way. We need to evacuate the building as quickly as possible.'

Harry rushed forward to pick me up. The woman in the dress was pushing to get through the door as quickly as she could. But she wasn't going to get away from me this time.

So I leaped out of Harry's arms and threw myself at her.

She stamped on me again, piercing into me with her stiletto.

Pain seared through me once more, and I fell back on to the floor. My legs buckled underneath me.

And then the most unexpected thing happened. As Harry dived forward to try and protect me, there were more screams – this time from the woman – and then SHE crashed to the floor.

It was chaos, but in the melee I saw Dolby, Sepp, Spike and Petunia pulling her down.

They had all piled in to save me.

And then two things happened at the same time.

Firstly, Sourman, who had been trying to help the lady in the dress, got a blast of extra-hot chilli powder straight into his eyes. And you have never heard such a squeeeeal in your life.

What a baby HE is.

Secondly, a large blue crystal detached itself from the woman's dress and spun across the floor at the very moment her blonde glossy wig fell off.

And then I knew why her voice and her wig were so familiar. It was Nastasia Raven.

Chairman Pragnell was having a major tantrum as he somersaulted down the stairs in an all-out panic. His earlier calm had evaporated after he'd checked the Star of the Blue Moon on its cushion, only to discover it had been replaced by a piece of worthless crystal.

But his trained eye saw the real Star spinning across the marble floor as he arrived unceremoniously at the bottom step of the elegant stairway.

'My baby, what are they doing to you?' he cried, as he dived across the marble like a cat pouncing on a mouse.

Nastasia Raven gave the blinded Sourman a few digs with her stilettos in an attempt to get away – which made him yelp even more – but she was no match for Harry, who pinned her to the floor.

'Oi, I'm an actress!' Nastasia Raven protested.

'Aren't you just,' Harry said to her with a certain swagger to his voice. 'Well, you've just played your last part for a while.'

When we got back to the café in Bloomington, there was quite a reception committee waiting for us. Beanie puffed up my bed for me and curled up next to me so that she could give me a gentle hug.

The news about the attempted robbery had travelled to Bloomington faster than the internet could carry tins of meat – and there was big news on that front too.

In fact, Beanie was more interested in telling me about that. 'We've solved the mystery of the disappearing internet, Sammy. Those men we saw in the barn were internet pirates, and they were stealing video games and using up all the wires – or something like that. No ships or eye patches or anything, but still criminals. The police took them away.'

'Beanie, I think Sammy and Harry have more interesting things to tell us about than that,' Mrs Brown suggested. She seemed to be in a bit of a state.

'Sammy foiled the heist!' Harry told them triumphantly. But I wasn't in the mood for signing autographs just then. My injuries were aching like anything.

'None of the others could have picked up the scent of the Star of the Blue Moon,' Harry said to Mrs Brown.

And thank goodness Harry had taught me to follow my instincts, so I picked up the bad vibes and observed what was going on around me, as well as using my nose.

Although my back was hurting a lot, I was rather enjoying being nursed by Beanie – closely attended, I might add, by Robin. He'd been the first to get to the village green because he heard the helicopter coming about three minutes before everyone else.

Then Farmer Gerald, Dr Parkin and Mrs Muggins arrived to hear what had happened. They ate their way through a whole tray of Jammy Dodgers, straight out of the oven and smelling nice – one of Beanie's mixtures, made when her hands had dodged being washed first.

And I just felt well enough to have a bowl of

tripe, which, of course, I shared with my BDF Robin.

Everyone wanted the full story. Mrs Brown was still quite cross with Harry about my injuries, but she didn't want to miss anything either.

'How on earth did that ghastly woman get her hands on the Star of the Blue Moon when it was being so closely guarded?' Mrs Muggins wanted to know.

'Well, even though Chairman Pragnell had his best security man, who never blinks, beside the diamond, the guard got distracted. If someone dropped a silver tray of drinks behind us now, we'd all look over to see what the noise was about, wouldn't we? Even just for a second. And that's all it took for Nastasia Raven to switch the Star of the Blue Moon with a fake, which she took from the decoration on her dress.'

'So the waiter was part of the plot too, was he?' Gerald asked.

'Good lord, no,' Harry said. 'There were five women in on it. Turns out they're a gang that has pulled off a lot of robberies. We think they were on their way back from another heist in Paris when Sammy sensed something was wrong about them in the VIP suite at Heathrow.'

'The Pink Panthers, I think you'll find they're called,' Dr Parkin said.

'Exactly,' Harry confirmed, pointing at Dr Parkin as if he was the star pupil in class. 'All of them masters of disguise. One of them knocked the tray of drinks out of the waiter's hands to create the diversion; two of them stood with Nastasia close to the Star of the Blue Moon to block any cameras; and the last one let off a smoke bomb in the ladies' loo.'

'Why bother?' Mrs Brown asked. 'Why didn't Nastasia just leave quietly with the Star of the Blue Moon hidden on her dress?'

'Well, the more chaos there was, the more likely

they were to get away. And it made it much harder for Sammy to sniff out the Star of the Blue Moon amongst a crowd of people all rushing to leave at the same time.'

'Oh, you're such a clever dog,' Beanie said, giving me a kiss. I blushed quite a bit.

The truth of it is that Nastasia Raven might well have got away if it hadn't been for the rest of the team piling in and backing me up. It was a strange thing that . . . Why had the others in the Border Security Dog Unit changed their attitudes towards me?

Why was I suddenly one of them when they hadn't let me into their friendship group to start with?

Well, even though I'm now part of their gang, I would never exclude anyone like they did at the beginning. And NOT that I'm going back to the

Border Security Dog Unit either.

Just then something very unexpected happened. The door of the café burst open and in walked Chairman Pragnell, his hair flowing in the air.

Harry introduced him to Mrs Brown. She was a bit cool with him at first. I think she blamed him for my injuries. But eventually she offered him a Jammy Dodger, which he declined because, he said, his body was a temple. That must be rather uncomfortable . . .

But it turned out that I was the purpose of his visit, which was rather good.

'Sammy,' he cried, throwing himself on to his knees in front of me. 'Are you all right?'

I gave him a so-so look.

'Sammy, you saved the day. You saved the Emporium from the most terrible disgrace. We would have been the laughing stock of the diamond world if you hadn't saved us.'

Harry shuffled forward in case Pragnell wanted to say something nice about him too.

'Oh, it's all part of a day's work,' Harry said, crouching down next to us. 'Isn't it, Sammy?'

Well, it was easy for Harry to say that. His back hadn't been punctured by one of Nastasia Raven's giant stiletto heels. That was very much NOT part of a day's work, as far as I was concerned. I just cocked my head to one side.

'Sammy, I have a small reward for you – a little something from the Emporium to say thank you,' Pragnell said, as he swept his bouffant hair back. He theatrically removed a package from his pocket with a flourish of his hand, and there before my eyes was a diamond-studded dog collar.

'I had this made for Crown Prince Hans of Estonia's greyhound, but he can wait,' Pragnell announced to the crowd in the café, as if he was on stage at the London Palladium. And he placed the beautiful collar round my neck.

'You are now the most lavishly collared dog in the world, Sammy.'

Well, thank you very much, I tail-wagged. The collar was rather beautiful. And not too heavy. But the best bit was that it had a lovely strong melted-cheddar-cheese smell.

REALLY PUNGENT.

'We can't possibly accept that,' Mrs Brown said quickly.

I wasn't so sure we couldn't, so I gave Beanie a knowing look.

'Well, Mum, I don't think Chairman Pragnell is giving it to you. It's a gift for SAMMY and she seems quite happy,' Beanie told her mother firmly.

I gave my tail another good wag just to make sure Harry got the message too.

'But what if it gets lost or stolen?' Mrs Brown asked.

'Oh, don't worry about that,' Pragnell said confidently, leaping up to his full height and raising his eyebrows at Harry. 'It contains a hidden tracking device. You don't think I'd let this number of diamonds go galloping through Estonia round the neck of a greyhound without knowing exactly where they were going, do you?'

And with that he gave me a lovely kiss. Then he disappeared out of the door in a whoosh, just like a superhero.

Eventually Robin and the locals all went home, after they'd taken it in turns to inspect my beautiful new collar. But Harry, who isn't a local, remained in Mrs Brown's most comfortable chair and didn't look like he was going anywhere.

I was very happy about that, so I limped over and put my head in his lap. And Beanie came and sat on the floor next to me and gave me a stroke.

'Harry's car's broken down again,' Mrs Brown said to Beanie. 'So he's going to stay for a few weeks, just until he gets it sorted out. And he can help me with our online bakery business.'

Everyone seemed quite happy to hear that news. And if Harry was happy to stay, then so was I! We'd come on a long journey from Primrose Hill via Harry's house and Heathrow Airport. It was time for this lucky puppy and Beanie to concentrate on our famous bureau of investigation from now on.

ACKNOWLEDGEMENTS

Grateful thanks to all of the fantastic team at HarperCollins *Children's Books*: Nick Lake, Megan Reid, Charlie Redmayne, Cally Poplak, Kate Clarke, Elorine Grant, Eve O'Brien, Hannah Marshall, Jane Baldock, Deborah Wilton, Nicole Linhardt-Rich and Tanya Hougham. Thanks to Steve May for the wonderful illustrations. Thanks to my copy editor Sarah Hall and my proof reader Mary O'Riordan.

These are the memoirs of Holly Hopkinson, aged ten — except without any of the rubbish adults usually put in, thank you very much.

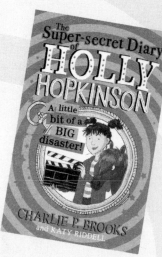

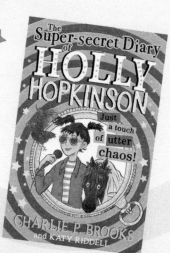